Sto

TIME:110100

The bells of the crown are being stolen by bandits. I must follow the sound.

From *Farewell, Angelina*
by Bob Dylan

TIME:110100

LEO P. KELLEY

WALKER AND COMPANY
New York

First published in the United States of America in 1972 by the Walker Publishing Company, Inc.

Published simultaneously in Canada by Fitzhenry & Whiteside, Limited, Toronto.

ISBN: 0-8027-5551-8

Library of Congress Catalog Card Number: 71-186186

Printed in the United States of America.

1687079

To my mother
and the memory
of my father.

Chapter 1

HE LAY MOTIONLESS and emptied of dreams in the narrow crystal prison encasing his naked body. His eyes were closed. His black hair curled down around his shoulders and beyond. His finger and toenails curled also, the blunt blades of organic scimitars.

He did not—could not—see the white knife of lightning slice the sky outside the room in which his prison was housed. The thick voice of the thunder that followed the sky's illumined sundering sounded but he slept on undisturbed.

Later, when the great tree outside the building split at the lightning's electric touch and added its own protesting voice to blend with that of the uncaring thunder, he slept on. As the tree shuddered, leaned, and then crashed against the building, he did not stir.

The weight of the fallen tree's branches caused the door of the building to bulge inward and then burst open to admit the cold rain.

Almost immediately a great black bird, its wings fluttering wetly, flopped through the door. Its beak opened to permit its protests to invade the clean silence of the room in which it unexpectedly found itself. Water dripped from its ebony body as it found its feet and scrabbled across the floor on talons as thin as threads. It spread its wings and shook them, then turned its head and pecked forlornly at its feathers, a damp and useless preening.

It bent its legs and settled slowly on the closed trapdoor set in the floor, its glittering eyes glowing like the raindrops that glistened on its body. One of its eyes closed and then quickly opened again as the thunder uttered another incomprehensible sentence.

Time passed.

The sleeper in the crystal casket saw no bird.

The bird in its search for sleep saw shapes within the room which its tiny brain could not comprehend.

Both bird and sleeper existed in their separate worlds as outside the building the rain slowed and finally stopped. Silence returned to the room and the two living creatures slept, each unaware of the other, each sheltered from the world outside the room and whatever that world might hold for them.

The sound, when it suddenly came, was like a shrill whistle formed by invisible lips. In its shrillness, however, there seemed to lurk the dark sound of a statement—as well as the much darker sound of a summons.

The bird screeched several times, an abrupt and terrified anthem, and was suddenly aloft in the still air. Flying without direction, responding to the biological warnings of its alarmed body, it swooped first one way and then wheeled sharply to career crazily in the opposite direction.

As the white lights flickered into life on the screen that formed one entire wall of the odd room, the bird screeched again, its voice an anxious wail.

Wings awhir, it looped backward suddenly. As it did so, one of its wings caught in the web of thin cables suspended from ducts set in the ceiling. Frantically the bird struggled to free itself—and failed. It

2

hung there a moment, its dark breast pulsing, its eyes clamped shut, and then it fluttered once more but to no avail. Hopelessly trapped, the wire wound among the feathers and slender bones of its wing, it hung, breathing soundlessly.

The bird's struggles had torn loose the end of the conduit that entered the crystal casket of the sleeping man. Now it dangled loosely inside the casket, no longer attached to the skull of the sleeper. Only a thin film of red paste on the man's forehead indicated where the conduit had once been connected to him.

The bird shuddered helplessly in its trap and twirled about, suspended between floor and ceiling.

At last, when it could muster no more energy to struggle with the cord, that had caught it and halted its frightened flight, the bird let itself hang limply, its head down, its body swaying slightly.

Below it in the crystal casket, an eye opened. And then a second eye. They closed, only to slowly open again. At the sides of the no longer sleeping man, his fingers flexed.

The bird stared down.

The man stared up at it, his eyes moving slightly from side to side as they dumbly measured the diminishing arc described by the black body swaying above him.

As his fingers touched his thighs, the man became conscious of them and of the smooth contact of flesh with flesh. He touched all ten fingers to his two thighs and then experimentally pressed first one finger, then another and another against his legs. As he did so, his eyes continued their left-right-right-left tracking of the trapped bird.

Slowly, his right hand rose to touch the thin crystal of the arched lid of the casket in which he was lying. He turned his attention from the bird to his hand, watching it move along the glass. He heard the faint *ting* as the pressure of his hand pushed the lid of his casket up an inch. His tongue moved in his mouth. He felt it pressing against his teeth and then moving past his lips. In mute wonder, he watched both of his hands lift the lid of the casket. When it lay back on its hinges, he lowered his hands and fumbled with the cilia-like filaments that were mindlessly massaging the muscles of his body. When he had freed himself of them and their ministrations, he concentrated on directing the actions of his body. It took him some time to manipulate it properly so that he could sit up. And then much more time was spent in learning to control the mechanism of himself sufficiently so that he could climb, somewhat clumsily, out of the casket.

The bird gave a thin cry as, a moment later, the man lurched to one side and then slid to the floor; he spent the next several minutes touching his toes, his testicles, and other parts of his body, which he obviously found fascinating.

Tentatively, he rose to his feet again, holding tightly to the rim of the casket for support. He became aware of tensions in various parts of his body. Muscles strained as he stretched. Ligaments grew taut, and bones clicked beneath their covering of flesh.

The bird opened its beak and emitted a sound that was louder than a chirp but not quite a shriek.

He stared up at it in wonder. As he reached up to touch it, the bird's body came alive and it fluttered, an ebony bundle of agitation, seeking desperately to avoid his touch. But he gripped it in his hands and felt its warmth. One of his thumbs rested against its breast. He felt its heart drumming. He held the bird in one strong hand and placed the other against his own chest to feel the beating of his own heart. Vaguely sensing a kinship with the creature he held in his hands, he began to unwind the cord that had captured it. When he had succeeded in freeing it, he set the bird gently down on the floor and was both startled by its sudden lifting into the still air and surprised at its sudden disappearance through the partially open door.

Alone, he looked about the room, which was constructed of an unseamed material. The low ceiling arched slightly; the walls curved outward beneath it. The overall impression the room gave was that of a well-lighted tunnel, but no single source of illumination was visible. The light seemed to ooze through the material of which the structure was built. There seemed to be no furniture, nor were there windows. Color was absent. The ceiling, the walls, and the floor had the pallor of frost.

As he stared about him, he noticed other caskets resting on raised pallets not far from one wall. They formed a neat, almost regimented line. Placing one foot in front of the other and paying careful attention to the act he was performing, he walked toward the mounds of crystal.

As he reached the first one, he bent forward slightly and peered down at the woman it contained. Her eyes were closed as his had been only minutes earlier. Her skin was pale. He noted the curves and gentle roundings of her naked body, so unlike the angularities and planes of his own. Staring dully at the woman beneath the gleaming glass, he sought to make sense of her presence there as well as his own. No clear thoughts came to him. No answers reached him; he did not know how to ask the correct questions.

The next casket contained another woman, shorter than the first. Her graying hair was curled and her features were coarse. Her large nose was soft, its wide nostrils fleshing it out even further. Her mouth was a thin line bisecting an austere face. Her cheeks were plump puddings beneath her forehead.

He returned to the casket containing the other woman. Yes, he preferred to look at her.

But not at the thin cable that was fastened to the center of her forehead. Without fully realizing what he was doing, he raised a finger to touch his own forehead, where traces of ointment remained. He could see pink beads of the same ointment surrounding the conduit at its point of contact with the woman's forehead.

More quickly, he moved down the line of caskets. An old man, bearded. A young man, also bearded, with a superbly developed body and the ghost of a grin raising the corners of his mouth. Others. Eight in all. And all with conduits reaching down from separate ceiling ducts to enter their caskets and make contact with the skin covering their skulls.

Puzzled, the man stood without moving, looking from one casket to the next. He became aware of the silence in the room and found himself thinking of the bird he had freed. He was vaguely sorry it was gone. He turned to stare at the door through which it had disappeared. He took a step in the direction of the door and then a second step.

But he halted abruptly when he heard the sudden shrilling that pierced the silence and his mind as well. Throwing up his hands to cover his ears, he stood still, his head lowered.

The sound ceased.

He looked up and saw the flickering lights that appeared on the screen following the cessation of the sound. Fascinated by their cavorting images, he moved toward them. When he reached the screen, he raised his hand to touch them. His fingers collided with a thick sheet of glass beneath which the lights flickered and flashed.

His lips parted as he smiled stiffly.

The exotic spectacle continued to amuse and fascinate him. At last, he gave up trying to grasp the images between his fingers. He simply stood in front of the screen and gazed at their odd shapes, concentrating first on one, then on another, as a message marched, fragmented by his erratic and uncomprehending attention, past his eyes . . .

. . . *repeat . . . reconstruction continues . . . chosen method . . . only one feasible . . . artifacts have been destroyed . . . to reduce risk of . . . disposition of nine to be determined based on evidence accumulated . . . electronic monitoring . . . Helen . . . New York . . .*

The words alive in the lights intrigued him. Their shapes, curved or starkly angular, delighted him. And yet . . . And yet, as he watched the gaily glittering words, there was something—something that stirred in his brain like a hunted animal darting from thicket to thicket, now almost visible, a moment later merely another shadow among a confusion of swiftly shifting dark shapes.

One word among all the others acted as a blunt dart flung at his memoryless mind. *Nine.* But what did it mean? He traced the outline of the word on the glass shielding it from his touch. *Nine.* He opened his lips, placed his tongue against his teeth and spoke the word aloud. "Nine." A feeling of fury welled up within him. His saying of the word had not worked the sought-after magic. Vaguely, he recognized the word as a symbol for a number. He leaned his forehead against the cool glass, closed his eyes and then opened them quickly as the whistle sounded again.

Startled, he withdrew and stared up at the electric words. He watched them flow to the right and then vanish from the screen. For a moment, only blankness met his gaze. And then, when the sound ceased, other words eased across the screen in a brilliant track; a few attracted his attention, most of them escaped it completely.

. . . authority hereby granted . . . to make independent and unilateral decision concerning permanent disposition . . . based on data . . . decision is scheduled for Time: 110100 . . .

He took a step backward and then another, his arms at his sides. He watched the words repeat themselves. He barely heard the sound of the whistle that seemed to initiate the flow of language. For uncounted minutes he stood watching without understanding anything of what he saw on the illumined slate of symbols. Finally, becoming bored with the display, he turned away as the screen said, *Time: 108016.*

He walked slowly toward the crystal casket of the first woman, the one he liked to look at. For a time, he stood staring down at her body, watching her breasts rise and gently fall. And then he became aware of what he at first believed to be another occupant of the casket. It took him some time to realize that what he saw was his own reflection in the glass. He examined the bearded man suspended halfway between himself and the woman enclosed in her glass prison.

He did not recognize the stranger. The color of the

stranger's hair—black—was somewhat familiar but its length puzzled him. The frown on the face of the man staring up at him made three creases in the flesh between his thick eyebrows. It was a fairly young face, but the frown it wore added fictitious years to it. Did he like the face? The answer to his question fled as he raised his hands and they obliterated the image in the glass. Removing his fingers from his face, he looked once more at the man in the glass.

Who?

No name came to him.

He moved to one side. So did the man in the glass. He grimaced, baring his teeth. So did the man in the glass. He winked. His wink was returned.

Me, he thought. But—.

Who?

The single syllable of his question alarmed him. It whispered of a life without coordinates, an identity without focus. He could not remember his name or where he was or, more importantly, why he could not remember. He felt no pain. But he did feel—he could not name the emotion that chilled his naked skin and dried the saliva in his mouth. A faint moan slipped through his lips and quickly faded into silence.

Below him, the woman's breasts lifted, lowered, lifted again.

He touched the lid of her casket. If he had opened his prison, he could, he believed, also open this one. He lifted the lid an inch and as he did so the conduit tore free of its mooring against the woman's forehead.

The sudden sound of singing outside the building caused him to stiffen and then to spin around toward the source of the sound. He stood motionless for a moment, his fists clenched and his teeth grinding relentlessly against one another.

"—and the wicked wiggle in her walk makes her tits twinkle!"

As he listened to the somewhat harsh voice merrily extolling the physical attributes of a woman as enterprising as Eve and as elusive as a will o'the wisp, his curiosity concerning the singer drowned his earlier anxiety.

Forgetting the casket in which the woman was lying motionless, he began to move toward the door that had been torn open by the falling tree. When he reached it, he awkwardly eased his body past the branches that fingered their way into the room. Drooping leaves swept his face as he climbed over the slanting tree trunk. Shards of loose bark scraped his unclothed body.

He emerged from the wet womb of the tree and stood staring at the vast world surrounding him and stretching away into an unmeasurable distance. Far from him mountains rose, their summits swathed in soft crowns of pale mist. Trees stood tall above their roots that were sunk firmly into grassy ground, their leafy eyes on a sky they seemed to seek to touch. Green was the dominant color of the landscape. Green were the swords of grass beneath his feet. Green too were the faintly veined vines climbing the walls of the building from which he had emerged.

Lazing in the blue sky were clouds, sisters of the mists resting on the mountaintops, their whiteness made brighter by the dazzling gaze of the sun which now shared the sky with them.

He halted, folding his arms about his body despite the warmth that was everywhere, and stared at this world he had discovered. All that lay before him bruised his eyes with an easy but disordered beauty.

He started as a small animal leaped from some bushes nearby and bounded away, its white tail pom-pomming above its sleek buttocks. And elsewhere, everwhere, birdsong. Threads of sound unwound in the pleasant air as invisible birds in their unseen nests gossiped together about food and the rich feel of air sliced thin by wings.

Blending abruptly with the vibrant bird chorus was a vulgar burst of words . . .

"I'll slip my sword in your sheath, and we'll let the sweet battle begin, oh, my lovely little lady . . ."

The singer sat perched on the limb of a tree, like a male bird of gaudy plumage. The naked man examined the one-piece suit of golden fabric that the singer wore. It matched almost perfectly the tawny splendor of the body it covered. The singer, the naked man slowly sensed, was not—what? Not like him.

The difference between them dwelled in a certain stiff regularity of the singer's movements, an obviously ordered set of discrete actions that combined to produce a single motion. Edging closer, the man saw that the singer serenading the unnamed woman was definitely different.

His skin was slick and unwrinkled. His ripe male laughter contained a hint of falsity, as if his merriment were manufactured and not the gay product of genuine emotion. His arms were bared by the garment he wore. He possessed shoulders any ox would envy. His chest was thick and mounded above his narrow waist and equally narrow hips. His arms were young oaks, his limbs lean and long. A stiff codpiece covered his genitals, calling attention to their immensity.

Brilliantined by the orange light of the sun that

11

was slipping lower in the sky, the treed singer caught sight of the naked man. His eyebrows lifted to loop above the wide blue of his eyes. He held out his arms as if in welcome, and when the naked man shrank back from the gesture, he leaped lithely down from the limb on which he had been sitting and slyly beckoned.

"I have a proposition for you," he called out, striding briskly toward the naked man.

The man ran.

The gilded singer promptly pursued and finally overtook his quarry. Gripping one of the man's arms, the no longer singing troubadour asked, "What's your name?"

No answer.

"Hey, man, you must have a name! They all had names. I remember that. What's yours?"

The naked man's low moan was his only answer.

"Hold it, friend. Let me check my memory transplant flow." The golden figure scratched his head in an oddly angular fashion and then swiftly turned an almost invisible jeweled wheel set behind one of his drooping ear lobes.

"Sam," he said after a moment. "Dog, Evelyn, Cisco, Christ, Eris, Ed, Smith." He gazed at his companion. "Do any of them sound familiar? No? Well, hell, then just pick one that sounds good to you. That's what all we simulacra did for ourselves in the beginning."

The naked man looked away, frowning. Then he gasped as he saw the figure splitting the skyline at the top of a nearby hill. It sat astride a blood-red horse bedecked with martial banners. In its hand a feathered lance thrust skyward. It wore brown leather garments bound by thongs and from its belt

12

dangled a jawless skull. Its white face brought a chill of fear to the naked man as his eyes traced the jagged lines of the figure's lips and met for one awful moment its dead black eyes.

"Never mind him," said the golden man when he noticed what had distracted his companion. "Pick yourself a name." He waited a moment and then, when he received no response, impatiently squeezed the man's arm.

But it was not this squeeze that ultimately elicited an answer. It was instead the abrupt disappearance from the hillcrest of the watching warrior that freed the naked man's tongue.

"Su-Smith?"

"Put it there, Smith!" exclaimed the simulacrum, seizing his companion's right hand and covering it with his left. "Pleased to meet you, Smith. How the hell do you do? You getting much these days?"

The handshaking, vigorous and prolonged, ended at last.

The man who had so suddenly become Smith reached out to touch the shining suit of the simulacrum facing him.

"You must have just been rousted," said the simulacrum, "by a husband home too soon. Am I right? Is that why you're running around like that with your balls all abounce?"

"Me—I—."

"I'll fix you up. We philanderers have got to stick together. Which reminds me. As I was saying a moment ago, Smith, I have a proposition for you."

"Prop-o-si-tion."

"Right on! You can consider me a connoisseur of clever delights. You might call me a banker whose accounts have such lovely names as Lilith and Elizabeth and Deirdre. When you see me in action, my man, you will know me for a master of lithe revels where the music is soft and the dance never ends and incense alters ordinary air, transforming it into a stoning wine. Now that I know your name, let me introduce myself. I am Superstud!"

Smith began to back away, his head moving almost involuntarily from side to side as he sought to comprehend the rapid flow of his mechanical companion's words.

"Hey, wait!" Superstud yelled after him. "You haven't even heard my proposition." When he had caught up with Smith and persuaded him to halt and at least listen, he continued, "I'm in the market for an assistant. You look like you could qualify."

Smith felt embarrassment at the glance Superstud shot at his groin.

"Yes, Smith, you definitely do qualify. You're young enough and lusty but not yet truly tested. I can tell. I can always tell. Now here's what and who I've got in mind."

Smith listened warily.

Superstud waved a hand in the direction of the lush vista of grass and trees stretching out before him and declared, "This garden may not be exactly or even entirely Edenesque but it is nevertheless a garden—a garden in which grow glorious girls and women alive with life. These females of which I speak—ah—they are the sweet flowers in a man's bouquet, and you and I, Smith—you and I together—can buzz among them, eager and obliging bees. You do follow me, don't you?"

"Nu-no."

The sigh from Superstud was more condescending than melancholy. "Come along then. Let's sit ourselves down here on the grass, and I'll go over things step by easy step. Now," he continued when they were seated facing each other in the faint gloom of the new evening, "I have a computer which—."

"A computer?"

Superstud patiently explained to Smith about computers. "The bouquet I've been speaking about—the flowers I mentioned earlier—they're all computerized. I mean, they're all taped. You can punch in your preferences. Do you like big boobs? Thin hips? A truly uninhibited head? Well, you put it all together and then you punch it all in and the computer will supply you with the magic name. Then—."

"Then?"

Superstud placed both hands between his legs, leaned back, and gave a moan of orgasmic ecstasy. "Then, Smith, let the jester withdraw and the torches be doused, for it is then that the real revels begin."

"Girls," Smith murmured, remembering, but not altogether clearly. "Women."

"This way. Follow me." Superstud's rising to his feet was a swaying, an unwinding of limbs until the virile sun of himself seemed to gild the darkening sky above Smith. He moved away, glancing back now and then and beckoning to Smith, who rose quickly but awkwardly to hurry after his nonhuman mentor.

Superstud talked as they walked past thick trees and drooping bushes. "—and she is absolutely tireless. *Tireless,* I tell you! All night long and all day too will she twist and contort to your heart's content. A cliché admittedly. But one that is appropriate to describe Jessamyn. Then there is Beth, who has been programmed to provide a vast catalog of what some might primly call peculiar pleasures. Her wardrobe alone will prime valves within you so that you will spurt magnificently before ever she places one of her fourteen fingers upon your body. Ah, you shall see! You will—it's just a bit farther on, just around—. *Here!*"

As Smith followed Superstud around the corner of a wild hedge that bore red and purple berries, he saw the computer of which the simulacrum had spoken. It stood facing him at the end of a triangular lane lined with flowers that the now-rising moon revealed as a waxen blue. The computer, at the apex of the triangular path, was glass-faced and electric-eyed. With a starlike constancy, it winked and blinked in its mechanical silence. The blue flowers nodded, ignoring it. It stared at Smith and Superstud, turning its wheels and faintly ticking.

Smith stared back at it.

Superstud folded his arms and nodded, a mute acknowledgment of Smith's evident awe. "The buttons there on the right are all labeled. March, my man! Choose the creature who will dim the moon tonight and give new meanings to words like love and desire."

Smith gave Superstud an uneasy glance.

"He who hesitates is—," Superstud said but did not finish his remark.

Lost.

Somewhere in Smith's brain memory stirred itself and tried to awaken, and the word resounded.

Lost.

The concept paralyzed him, but Superstud reached out and placed a heavy golden hand upon his shoulder, shoved, and Smith found himself trotting down the triangular path toward the expressionless face of the computer.

Superstud, laughing loudly, followed him. He gave Smith instructions. He told him how to operate the machine and read the names on the list behind the glass where wheels whirled. He read in a voice silken with enticements the descriptions that were linked to the names.

Smith said, "One?"

Superstud, roared his laughter into the night sky and shouted, "There are no limits to human love. I know that. I *remember* it. One? If one is all you want, then choose just one. But if a dozen or a score are more to your taste then by all means—. Yes, by all means. Pay no attention to mathematics or its complexities. In this game, any number can play, and one need not understand any equation other than that most intricate one that defines the fire blazing in the middle of every man's and woman's fleshy world."

Smith's index finger reached out to the button above which letters spelled: S-E-R-E-N-A. He knew nothing of the meaning of the letters and little about what Superstud's monologue had meant. But he did know enough. He knew what a girl was, what a woman looked like. As his finger made contact with the button's redness, he remembered the young woman in the casket, the one it had pleased him to watch as she lay sleeping beneath his gaze. The memory made him turn away from the computer, but not before his finger had caused the button to sink deeply into the slick panel.

He saw only the flat expanse of the path he had just traversed to reach the computer and the hedges, bushes, trees, and grass that grew everywhere in green abandon. Gone was the building in which he had just been reborn. Had it ever actually existed?

Had he really encountered the black bird in the strange room where the little lights created cryptic messages on a huge screen?

"His name is Smith!" Superstud declared.

Smith spun around to find Superstud pointing at him.

The female simulacrum standing beside Superstud wore a tunic of some sleek yellow fabric. Her hair was the color of woodsmoke. Her eyes sparked in the finely boned beauty of her young face. Her flesh was pale, as if powdered, and she stood in a way that lent a voluptuous topsy-turviness to the citadel of herself.

"Smith," she said, her voice the sound of a small animal emerging from hibernation. She stepped toward him, holding out one hand, its palm turned upward toward the stars.

Smith stood transfixed in the path.

She came toward him, moving through the night as if it were an essence she emanated, and took Smith in her slender arms. As her hands moved up and down the line of his spine, Superstud's laughter rollicked around them.

Chapter 2

SUDDENLY, SPLINTERING the sound of Superstud's raucous joy, came a cry that caused Smith to pull away from Serena. He looked about in the darkness as she reached for him again, and Superstud's laughter that had been a dam bursting became the faintly fluting sound of ripe grapes being pinched.

Smith saw the simulacrum who had cried out careening wildly down the side of the hill, in and out of the geometrically sharded moonlight, toward him and his two companions. He felt his skin grow taut as he stepped backward, his hands reaching behind him as if to clear his path, preparing for flight from the apparition that was swiftly bearing down upon him.

But Superstud stepped behind him and placed cold, golden hands on his shoulders, preventing further movement. Smith stood his ground as Superstud muttered, "It's Marsman. You saw him before—on the hilltop. He stalks the nights and hunts his enemies down the aisles of all the days. Pay no attention to him. Serena is waiting for you, my man. Already the hot juices of her body are flowing as she—."

"Stand and say!" bellowed Marsman as he reined his horse, and the white froth that roped along its black lips flew out to spatter Smith's face. "Say you, soldier! Be you friend or foe?"

Smith wiped the wet foam from his face as he stared up at Marsman's twisted mouth and gaunt cheeks.

"Speak!" Marsman shouted and slapped the flat of his feathered lance against Smith's ribs.

"I am Smith!"

"No ribbons on your brawny chest," Marsman observed in a voice that might have belonged to the skull swinging bluntly from the leather thong tied around his waist. "What campaigns have you planned? What conquests made?"

"I have no horse and no ribbons," Smith replied. "I awoke a little while ago and came out of the house where I had been sleeping—." His words, as he thoughtfully uttered them, had spaces between them. They dropped with his glance to the ground.

"What are your loyalties?" Marsman demanded. "What your allegiances?"

Superstud strode forward to confront Marsman. "Let him alone. Can't you see he isn't one of us?"

"He's one of them?"

"Obviously. Notice how he moves—like a perfectly designed and carefully engineered invention, not like us at all. Yes, he's definitely one of them and not a simulacrum."

Marsman's eyes flickered, two black fires in the roiling lava of his furious face.

Smith reached out a tentative hand, and the horse's rubine shoulder shivered violently at his touch, as it might at the sudden but delicate fall of a fly's feet on its sweating hide. He whispered something in the animal's erect ear.

"This, my horse," snarled Marsman, "has taken steel in its flanks and felt the fire of battle sear its

20

forelocks. A worthy beast. Fit to bear a fighter but not for much else."

"Its eyes—." Smith stood gazing into the moist brown pools.

"Its eyes? What about its eyes?" Marsman leaned over his saddle horn.

"So full of pain," Smith said to the horse, surprising himself.

A snort and a tossing of its head was the animal's answer.

"Smith!" Serena's cry was a counterpoint to the horse's sudden wild whinnying.

He turned as she allowed her tunic to slip to the ground. He watched her step out of the folds of cloth that shrouded both her ankles. He stared . . .

"Move on, Marsman!" Superstud shouted in glee. "The battle that is about to begin here is no concern of yours. It requires no courting of your consort, Death, nor does it seek to let blood loose to stain the soil. Beyond the next hill you may find what you need, Marsman. Perhaps there among scented clover you will find the enemy you require."

"Beware!" Marsman bellowed. "Do not mock war and its makers! Were it not for such as us you and all like you would perish with fire eating your lungs and the screams of your children your only dirge."

Marsman drew tight the reins in his hands, and the forelegs of his horse arced into the air. Blood freed by the rasping bit in the animal's mouth pinked the saliva drowning its great teeth. Down came its two hooves to crush the ground, and then it and its rider roared away up the side of a hill that seemed to tremble as it marked their passage.

"Forget him," said Superstud. "That," he pointed to Smith's erection, "is the only sword you will need here . . . . Serena!"

She moved slowly forward, stretching out her arms to Smith. His own arms rose slowly, and when his fingertips met Serena's, they both paused. A moment later there seemed to be but one body beneath Superstud's and the stars' eyes.

"Wait!" shouted Superstud suddenly. "Let others join their joy to yours!" He ran to the computer and pressed buttons at random, calling back names to Smith. "Gloria of the burnt butter skin. Beverly, come and bring your love that is a healing balm in Gilead. Tania! Jessamyn!"

From behind the computer they came, the swaying flowers, simulacra all, of which Superstud had spoken earlier with such enthusiasm. They glided into Smith's sight surrounded by soft orange clouds that stained the air with the scent of myrrh. They rode upon the backs of prancing pneumatic ponies and descended gracefully from the top of the computer on neatly knotted ropes of pastel polymers. Perfume came with them, drifting about their bodies and making sweet the deep night air. Amber rings flashed on their fingers, rich fireflies glittering gaily at Smith. Miniature bells rang non-canonical hours as they bounced above breasts both rouged and powdered, melodious chroniclers of the pleasures to come.

Superstud moved among them, a virile needle stitching an erotic fabric of loveliness, weaving a tapestry of sensual promises. Whispering first to one and then to another of the girls, so languid and yet so eager as they gazed at Smith, Superstud stoked their banked fires and fanned young flames into red and blazing life. Speaking happily to Smith, he called attention to the curve of a thigh, the thrust of a nippled mound of flesh. He shouted words and phrases as he patted buttocks and ran his golden fingers from the hill of a navel toward the feminine valley nestled between tense thighs.

Smith found himself drawn toward a girl whose slim body willowed in the moonlight spilling down upon it. She had the face of a wise child, all wide eyes—green—and a mouth that hinted faintly of decadence. Her light laughter was the sound of clouds colliding. Smith placed both of his hands against the flatness of his belly for a moment as if to prevent himself from escaping from himself, and then he was moving toward her as the other girls, aware that he had chosen, swirled about him, their fingers flicking against his skin, their eager words of encouragement a swarm of tantalizing butterflies softly assaulting his ears and arousing sleeping dreams within him.

As his body touched the girl's, he found he could not speak. He shuddered once as if a delicate whip had touched him—but all the girl had done was to rise up on her toes to place her lips on his while her legs parted slightly to admit him.

A moment later she was gone, running across the silvered grass, her companions urging her on and simultaneously calling out to Smith, telling him that he must pursue her, that nothing of value was won by the passive. Buffeted by the girls' warm words, he too ran. Behind him came the lovely pack, rippling with laughter, shepherded by Superstud whose cries of encouragement soon silenced all else.

"Wait!" Smith shouted, the word a loud insect seeking the bright light of the girl who was by now so far ahead of him.

"Jessamyn!" she called back to him.

"Jessamyn!" he cried, circling to one side as he sensed that she was about to turn.

Turn she did, and found herself captured by Smith in the way of an animal who knows that flight is useless and prefers capture to the hot bullets of its hunters.

When their kiss ended after scores of seconds, Jessamyn took Smith's hand in hers and led him farther into the bower surrounding them. Garlands of flowers hung above their heads. She reached up and plucked two buds. She tossed them to Smith who caught them and raised them to his lips. Then, reaching out to Jessamyn, he placed the two fragrant blooms in her blond hair, where they remained poised for an instant before falling gently to the ground at her feet.

"Smith," she murmured. "Love is loose in the night. Can you hear it mewing? Can you see its haunted face out there among the sheltering trees?"

"I can touch it," he answered, gripping her arms. "It feels as soft as—."

"As sea foam on a fiery ocean."

"Yes. I could drown in it."

"Come," she commanded and led him deeper into the bower.

They were alone now as they walked on together beneath the delicate flowers and the stars. Superstud had withdrawn. So had the girls. For a moment, Smith imagined the girls mounting their pneumatic ponies and climbing their ropes of pastel polymers to disappear like gusts of morning mist. He discovered that he could remember nothing of their faces. He could not recall their names. The world was all about him, but he and Jessamyn were its only inhabitants.

Moving along through it with Jessamyn, he heard drums beating and the sound of bare feet somewhere slapping the ground, practicing the intricate patterns of an unknown dance. He knew he was imagining it, calling up images both tender and bizarre as his body sent its secret signals to his brain and he shivered with an excess of emotional energy.

Drums.

No, one drum, he realized as he halted to listen.

Jessamyn, when she saw that he was listening to the deep and distant sound, relaxed and smiled at him. "It is only Marsman," she commented and placed her hands over her ears. When she took them away after the steady sound of the drumming had ceased, she added, "He beats his drum to summon armies. He sends out messages in the night to tell all those who dwell in the Valley of the Maimed that they must take up weapons else he and his mercenaries will spill their blood."

"Is he everywhere?"

"Marsman? It does seem so. His battles are many but his victories are empty triumphs."

"Empty?"

"What is emptier than death?"

Smith was not certain that he understood Jessamyn's question. Instead of answering it, he asked her a question. "Where is the Valley of the Maimed?"

She pointed, but her gesture told him nothing.

"What is it?"

"Don't you like me?" she inquired with a calculated pout.

Smith bent his head. His tongue circled the nipples on her breasts.

Jessamyn sighed, her head thrown back, her long hair hanging down her arched back as she abandoned herself to the sensation Smith was creating within her. A night bird awoke above them and gave one mournful cry before falling silent again.

On they walked until they came to a small lagoon that lay at the foot of a dashing waterfall. The scent of limes lay on the still air above the surface of the water. Smith seized Jessamyn and moved to pull her down beside him upon the mat of moss bordering the lagoon, but before he could do so she was gone from him. She raced to the edge of the lagoon and rose on her toes, her arms held high above her head, her palms touching. Then the arrow of her body sprang from an invisible bow and she was streaking downward. Her body split the smooth surface of the water and disappeared beneath it.

Smith rose and went to kneel at the edge of the lagoon, his nostrils filled with the bittersweet smell of the air. When she broke the surface of the water, Jessamyn drew back her dripping hair and called his name.

He dived into the water after her. But when he surfaced, she had vanished. Treading water, he looked about. She appeared briefly, only to dive down beneath the surface of the water a second time. He also dived and soon their two bodies came together in the silent world below the world.

For some time they swam, exchanging the roles of pursuer and pursued. Finally they emerged on the bank of the lagoon and lay down side by side, both of them breathless, both aware of the possibilities of their bodies, partly as a result of their recent joyous exertions.

Smith, when his lungs stopped heaving, seized Jessamyn and pulled her close to him. He did not speak as he covered her body with his own.

But Jessamyn spoke. Her words were breathy as if they came from some distant place within her. At last, she could utter no more words as her body lurched and writhed beneath Smith.

He felt the pressure building within him. He felt the blood beat through his body, a drum louder and more insistent than the one struck by Marsman, somewhere in the encompassing night.

The explosion of himself, when it came, was a violent cascade which Jessamyn received with a matching violence. Her buttocks rose from the ground as if they sought to rocket Smith into the sky that vaulted unseen above them.

"I love," Smith sighed after some time had passed, the sound of his voice bright in the dark air.

"But not me," Jessamyn said.

He ran his hand along her body, letting it come to rest between her thighs. Something in her remark had troubled him. He could not meet her gaze when he said, "Not you. But someone."

"Who?"

He shook his head. Her question left him confused. Anxious. Who indeed? There had been a girl in that old time before the time of his crystal casket, a girl he could not now remember, who had said the same words to him that Jessamyn had just used while they rode the stallion of their lust together. But her name was buried in the ruins of his mind where memory was an outcast. When he became aware of the wetness streaking his cheeks, he raised a hand and touched the thin rivers his eyes had released.

"Is she dead?" Jessamyn asked gently. "Humans die. Crutch told me that once. Is that why you weep? Because she is dead?"

"Yes. No. I don't know. I think—." The thought wouldn't come. Spent as he was, his past stolen by some unknown and unsuspected thief, Smith could only feel the pain that sliced his sinews as he struggled to remember the lost girl and his equally lost love for her.

"I'm sorry," Jessamyn whispered. "You humans are so—so—."

"Vulnerable." The word slipped unexpectedly from his lips.

"Vulnerable," Jessamyn repeated thoughtfully. "Yes, that is true. Like Loman.".

"Who is Loman?"

"One of us."

"A simulacrum?"

Jessamyn nodded. "He is almost as susceptible to sadness and pain as humans are. In fact, he is the most nearly human of us all."

"You mentioned someone named Crutch before," Smith murmured as sleep began to slip down upon him.

"Crutch is not whole. You are. So it is most unlikely that you will meet."

"I don't understand," Smith said, a note of desperation in his voice.

"Perhaps it doesn't matter," came Jessamyn's ghostly voice.

"It does matter. I know it does. I *have* to understand."

"Why? We are together."

"That isn't enough."

Jessamyn turned her head to one side. She moved her legs so that Smith's hand fell away from them.

He said, "I'm sorry."

"You're different from Superstud."

"I know."

She turned back to face him. "No, I don't mean just that he is a simulacrum like me. Not just that. I meant that he wants women the way a miser wants coins. There is no commitment involved, no surrendering of any part of himself. Superstud uses women without giving anything of himself to them. You shared yourself with me. I could feel it."

"I suppose it is the way I am. Why is Superstud the way he is?"

Jessamyn frowned and gnawed her lower lip. "It is the way he is made. His memories make him that way. He has no choice in the matter, none."

"Perhaps his experience—."

"When he was made—when Crutch, Marsman, Loman and all the rest of us were made—." She gave a little moan of distress. "Oh, I'm tired of talking. Take me."

But Smith was not tired of talking. He reached out and caressed Jessamyn's face. "Who made you all? Who made Superstud?"

"We don't know. He doesn't know. One day he didn't exist. The next day he did and he remembered wanting women. I remember nothing."

"Nothing?" shouted Superstud as he bounded into the glade and stood towering over Jessamyn and Smith. "Don't you remember the last time I sent you soaring, girl? You couldn't forget that!"

"I remember," Jessamyn admitted, her eyes on Superstud. "But that isn't the same thing. You remember things I can't even understand. It's different for you and Crutch—." Her voice faded.

"Superstud," Smith said, rising. "What do you remember?"

"Equations. Logarithms. How to plot the proper path for a bird to follow. Mozart. But most of all, moist female thighs and the twining together of tongues. I remember fucking and counting and that

29

only the fucking and not the mounting numbers mattered.''

Smith shook his head in bewilderment. Nothing that Superstud had said made any sense to him. What did equations have to do with women? When Superstud spoke of mounting numbers, did he mean the numbers of women he had taken in his time or did the numbers relate to the other, the equations? Smith felt again the thin despair that seemed to ferment in his bowels and boil up when he realized that not only did he not know who he was, he also did not know who—or what precisely—were the simulacra, seemingly the only other active inhabitants of this otherwise empty Eden. He recalled the caskets lying in the great hall. Were the sleepers confined within them also simulacra? There was no way of knowing for sure unless he could find his way back there and awaken one or more of them. But of one thing he was sure. He was not a simulacrum. His flesh was not like Jessamyn's. His was soft and pliable. Hers was taut and stiff. His body was warm; hers was cool. A pump labored in his chest, but from beneath Jessamyn's breasts came the dull *thrumming* sound that made him think of the computer that had so recently summoned her into his eager orbit.

"Are you spent?" inquired Superstud of Smith. "Or do you still have currency in reserve that you would be willing to invest?" Without waiting for a reply, Superstud hurried on. "I'll bring you a full bouquet, Smith. I'm sure Jessamyn has been delightful, but still she's only a single flower. To appreciate lilacs, one must learn about roses. To admire roses, one must know something of weeds. Ah, weeds! *Tania!*''

In response to Superstud's call, a black girl came

gliding into the bower and Superstud's open arms. They embraced. He told her what he wanted her to do, and she looked up at him, a smile of sharp white teeth and faintly glossy lips. The moment Superstud released her, she went and knelt in front of Smith. While Jessamyn, leaning back on her elbows, watched with unconcealed amusement, Tania followed Superstud's instructions, embellishing them with actions born of experience, sharpened by imagination, and stimulated by Smith's own responses. He found in his body a well of ecstasy that at times, as Tania dipped and rose above and about his body, bordered on a delicious agony.

As the minutes matured into hours, Smith alternately exulted and groaned from exhaustion. But whenever his exhaustion became apparent, one or another of the girls moving about in the sultry night would bend to him, would touch him here or taste him there so that his flaccidity would end as his phallus phoenixed upward to impale the stars.

Throughout the long night, as the moon moved on through the sky and then dropped down toward the horizon, Superstud would occasionally call for an intermission in the gamboling and the games in which he, like Smith, was vigorously engaged. During these respites, he talked to Smith. He told him that nothing mattered, nothing other than sex. Sex, said Superstud, was both the beginning and the end. It was the ripe fruit on which a man must feed if he was to live fulfilled. Chastity, he mused at one point, lying on his back while Tania sat waiting cross-legged at his side in earnest silence, was the fruit of a poisoned tree. Celibacy, he claimed, was the only perversion, insofar as it denied the essential nature of man. Would Smith willingly and knowingly choose never to bend his fingers? Smith said, no, he would not so choose. Why then, asked Superstud, should he deny the sultry demands made by his genitals? Was not the first action—the refusal to bend one's fingers, a perverted act in that it denied nature and the intent of nature's clever engineering? Yes, Smith agreed, it could be so called. Then, Superstud insisted, so was celibacy a perversion. Bodies were made to be enjoyed. They were, he argued, the source of all surcease and all pleasure.

"Then you must often fall in love," Smith remarked when Superstud finally paused to draw a deep breath.

Superstud's eyes, which he had closed in lazy contentment, opened at once. "In love? Me? Yes, I suppose that once upon a time I needed to call my behavior falling in love. But such talk is but a shadow upon the face of truth. Men talk of love when they need to deny what they consider the grossness of their appetites. They say they love in order to dwarf their towering guilt about sex. *Love!* Love is the pigment with which an untalented artist transforms the lily into something hideous and artificial. Better, I say, to let the lily live in naked splendor than to unnecessarily gild it. No, Smith, I think I have never been in love if the truth were to be told, which it so seldom is even among friends. I have merely cared for my garden. I prune a branch here—," Superstud touched Tania's navel, "—bend a stalk in a more desirable direction—," he ran smooth fingers down Jessamyn's arm and received her smile, "—and let desire germinate under the hard winds and soft rains I bring down upon my flowers."

"I remember—," Smith began and then, frowning, fell silent.

Superstud sat up. "You remember? What do you remember?"

"She said she loved me. I'm sure she did. I can almost remember her."

"Forget her. Touch Tania. Say sweet words to Jessamyn. Memory is a dusty trunk that is better left locked. Spiders spin in its dark interior, and their webs are strong enough to catch the unwary. Then, once caught in the web, down the steel strands comes the spider to sting. Smith, Jessamyn and Tania are here now. They are real. Take them. Let memories lie at peace in their graves."

"But she was—."

"I warn you, Smith."

"What is wrong with remembering? You said you remember things."

"I had no choice. I was made to remember."

"I don't know what you mean."

"Nor do I, my man. It is simply the way of things. When pleasure is present for the taking, questions only confuse issues. To enjoy is all."

"Superstud—." Smith wrapped his arms around his body as if seeking shelter from a cold wind.

"Yes?"

"What do you remember?"

"Women. I told you that."

"That's all?"

Superstud raised his arms and stretched languidly. "Isn't it enough?"

"For you, maybe. But what I don't understand is why you remember only women. Is there nothing else that you can recall? No other events or incidents?"

Superstud idly scratched his knee. He shook his head. "For me, memory is mainly a list of names, a catalog of nights and afternoons of pleasure. And yet—."

"And yet?" Smith prompted, leaning forward slightly as Superstud's eyes narrowed and his brow wrinkled.

"Sometimes I hear music. Sometimes symbols shake themselves free of the spiders' webs, and I think of the elegance lying in the heart of numbers. But such thoughts—such recollections—are only distractions from my primary concern. Nothing more than that. What I am trying to say—I am trying to say to you that my distractions are no more important to me than the thoughts of peace that occasionally occur to Marsman. When he speaks of them, it is as if they belonged to someone else entirely."

"For you, it is women," Smith mused. "For Marsman, it is—."

"War and its glories," Superstud interrupted. "But we have talked enough. Words weigh upon us. Get up, Smith. Shake yourself and send all your words tumbling away and out of sight. The night is not yet ended although the moon looks weary as it descends the sky. Come!"

Superstud's. last word, a command that ripped through the night, brought girls rushing toward him. Jessamyn was on her feet and dancing. Tania clasped Smith's hand and whirled about with him, laughing and urging him on to eager excesses.

Whips appeared in the hands of some of the girls. Flowers sprouted in their scented hair. The sibilant sound as the little whips touched Smith's body blended neatly with the notes from the flute at the lips of the young girl darting in and out of the bushes bordering the glade.

Jewels flashed on feet and fingers.

34

Juices flowed between Smith's body and the bodies of the simulacra—salt sweat, hot dots of blood released by teeth and nails, fluids erupting from hidden places, the vaguely acrid scent of lubricating oil, perfumes. 1687079

Bare feminine feet appeared wearing laced shoes with heels many inches high. Sleek furs flashed in hands and wrapped about writhing loins.

Feathers flared about a fire Superstud had set blazing beside the lagoon in which its reflected flames leaped.

Jessamyn bounded into the arena, chains weighing down her body, taunting Smith and telling him in wild words that bound as she was, so was she helpless, while his hands were free to inflict . . .

Tania handed him her braided whip.

Smith felt his arm rise, the whip arcing into the air. He heard the sound of its slap, heard Jessamyn scream, saw the smile that lent the lie to her agony. He watched as she dropped to her knees at his feet, her head bent forward, her long blond hair billowing out and down to hide her face, her hands in the black iron bracelets raised to him in silent supplication . . .

The scene before him—the raging fire, the chains, the fur, feathers, and leather whips—roiled in his mind, a scenario of broken images. Jessamyn was begging him not to strike her again and yet he heard the yearning lurking in her tone. He felt Tania's hands everywhere upon and within him. He existed as the whip Jessamyn waited for. He was the metropolis being plundered by Tania as she urged him on to odder delights.

He was—.

Who?

The word screamed in his mind. He dropped the

35

whip and seized Tania. With one thrust of his arms, he sent her toppling to the ground. Superstud sprang toward him but Smith's fist reached Superstud's jaw and the simulacrum crumpled, fell, and was quiet.

Smith wiped the sweat from his face and rubbed his eyes. Turning, he caught sight of his reflection in the surface of the lagoon. Flames seared the image. A demon stared back at him, its eyes as demented as the flames themselves, its flesh a dirty, sweat-slicked grotesquerie.

He screamed.

And then he turned away from the face in the water and began to run, his arms flung out in front of him, his heart beating an irregular rhythm. Through the night and past the trees, he ran, saliva slivering down into his beard. No one pursued him although he thought he heard Superstud shout a warning, but it might have been only a bird high in one of the trees crying out in feathered dismay.

He ran for uncounted minutes without direction and yet in search of something he could not at first name. But then, as his pace slowed, he realized that he was in pursuit of himself.

At last, totally exhausted, he slumped to the ground on the crest of a hill he could not remember climbing. Unconsciousness came to him, drowning his mind in black and purple shrouds.

When he awoke some time later, it was to feel something prodding his body. His eyes opened and he saw only dirt and flattened grass. It took him several seconds to realize that night had fled and that the sun once more ruled the domain of the sky. Stiffly, he turned as the dull prodding continued, wanting only to sleep, to forget.

At first, his vision somewhat blurred, Smith

thought the simulacrum standing above him was three-legged. But then, as his eyes focused, he saw that what he had thought was the man's third leg was wooden—a crudely carved crutch with which the simulacrum had been gently prodding him.

"What's the matter with you?" the man asked Smith, leaning heavily on his crutch. His voice was flat and without any trace of nuance.

"I—I'm all alone," Smith heard himself answer.

"Oh," the man breathed, shaking his head in sympathy. "I didn't realize that you were crippled too. Some hurts are hidden. But since you are damaged, come with me. I'll take you to a place where your injury will not be noticed."

"Where?"

"To the Valley of the Maimed. There we are all cripples and so no one notices deformities. There we are all alike and therefore normal. You can lean on me if you like. I'm stronger than I look. But first— aren't you cold?"

Smith glanced down at his unclothed body. Before he could respond to the simulacrum's question, he was handed a pair of green velvet trousers, a pink shirt of some soft material, and sandals made of leather straps adorned with living flowers—all of which the simulacrum had taken from the knapsack on his back.

Smith put the clothes on and then, leaning lightly on his new companion's shoulder, walked down with him into the crannied Valley of the Maimed.

Chapter 3

As the pair made their way down the hill, two pilgrims seemingly sharing the search for a single Grail, the simulacrum's withered leg dragged, shuffled. Clumps of wild grass detoured it, causing it to swing to one side. Half-buried stones trapped it briefly but it always managed to escape and lurch along, a single beat behind its brother.

Smith surreptitiously examined his companion as they walked. The simulacrum's face was round and drowned in wrinkles that seemed to be engraved upon the skin. His nose was his most prominent feature—the great beak of an eagle without such a beak's sharp edges. His green eyes sat deep in folds of flesh and sent out steady signals of distress that were the siblings of pain. His body was thick and short, as if two gigantic hands had simultaneously clasped the top of his head and both soles of his feet and then idly pressed, causing what once might have been a long, lean frame to coalesce into this square and heavy block of a body. Black hairs curled out of his ears and made of his eyebrows two unkempt bushes.

A pair of bright blue shorts of some coarse material covered his loins. Stopping midway down his thighs, they seemed to dramatize his afflicted limb. A blue shirt covered his upper body. It was held together in the front by one button and four safety pins. The shoes on his feet were clumsy items of uncured leather; the one on the left that hid his twisted foot was a miniature version of the other.

"My name is Crutch," the man told Smith. "That's what I call myself."

Smith murmured someething, a sound without consonants.

"I'm *Crutch*," the man repeated.

Smith became aware that the remark was designed to elicit a similarly informative response from himself. He said, "I call myself Smith. But that isn't my real name."

"How do you know it isn't?"

How did he know? "Well, it just doesn't sound exactly right. Or feel right either. But Superstud gave it to me."

"He didn't want it anymore?"

"I beg your pardon?"

"Your name—Smith. If Superstud gave it to you, he must have had no further use for it. Which makes sense. He has his own name. As I have mine. Both carefully selected. But yours is appropriate because it's a typical human name. I wouldn't ever expect to meet a horse with that name, but I'm not a bit surprised to meet a human being named Smith. Horses, if I remember correctly, are named Dobbin or Brownie. Something like that anyway. But humans were always a bit more complex in their nomenclature. I remember they used to talk about protective reactions and overkill. You know?"

"No, I don't know."

"You probably never will either. Where have you

been all this time? I never saw you around here before."

"Asleep. There was a house—a big building. A bird flew into it and something happened to me because it did. I woke up. There were others there with me."

"Others? Like you?"

"I really can't say for sure if they were exactly like me. I was confused at the time."

"Didn't you check?"

"There wasn't time. Superstud came and—."

"If you'd taken the time to check, you might not now be crippled like all the rest of us here in the Valley."

"You mean—?"

"I mean you might not be all alone if the others had been human too. You might have made a friend. Maybe even gained a lover. But what's done is done."

"I'm lost," Smith said. "I don't know where that building is. I don't know how to find my way back to it."

"It's not really lost, because you remember it."

"Yes, I think I see what you mean."

"I remember desks with papers all over them. Important papers. I hear telephones ringing.

They had reached the bottom of the hill and begun to walk across the floor of the valley when the sound of music reached Smith.

"That must be Superstud," Smith said. "One of his girls played a flute."

"It isn't Superstud," Crutch said emphatically. "Although he certainly does belong down here with the rest of us."

"Here? In the Valley of the Maimed? Superstud?"

"Some people go through life without ever know-ing they are crippled. Superstud is like that. He func-tions mainly on one level—the phallic. Such limited functioning is definitely that of a cripple. He'll join us here one day, you can be certain of it."

Great caverns opened their mouths everywhere about the Valley. Smith stared into them but saw lit-tle. Once he thought he saw a fire burning, but per-haps it was merely the sun's rays striking the mica that striated the rock formations. Crutch hobbled on ahead of him as if he were eager to reach a particular point at a particular time. Smith, as he walked, lis-tened to the music. It was both atonal and harsh, and yet it had a melody wrapped within its notes that was at one instant as sweet as honey and the next as bit-ter as an abandoned love.

Then from one of the caverns came a procession of people dressed in skirts of bright colors and trousers redolent with embroidery and sparkling sequins. But it was not the clothes the people were wearing which amazed Smith. It was instead the manner of their coming. Their parade was a clumsy kaleidoscope of movement. Men whirled in small circles, rapidly spinning the wheels of the chairs in which they sat. Other men beat drums with the stumps of handless limbs bound in rainbowed velvet. Women without legs were carried on litters, their voices loud with song and their eyes galloping gaily about among their companions. The few children among the throng were also damaged. A hermaphrodite led their little band, its boy-girl body lilting and swaying, its gauzy hair blowing in the breeze. Peg-legged men and women, merry as the madrigal they were all singing, pointed their wooden pegs, turned, swooped, and happily clicked their pegs' metal tips together in time and tune with the music played skillfully by fingers as dumb as their owner's lips.

No one fell. When one of the blind faltered, someone sighted would reach out a hand to guide the person onward. When one of the underlimbed would, in a too enthusiastic turn to the music, begin to topple, someone was there with a supporting body until the dancer's disequilibrium was gone. Wheelchairs whirled in and out among the dancers. Blind eyes sought the sun and found it because of the warmth it shed upon them. A hunchback bobbed among the crowd, a distorted cork on a never still sea.

"Why do they dance, Crutch?" Smith called out over the sound of the music. "How dare they?"

"How dare they indeed? When I was a child, I used to hide in the cool front parlor of our house where the shades were always drawn and dust was unimaginable. I used to peek through the spaces at the bottom of those always drawn shades and I would see the other children outside. They played, those children did. They never walked; they ran. To me, it seemed as if they flew across the asphalt and cement. They hopscotched. They hid and were found. They jumped ropes, climbed trees, hung upside down from bending branches, caught jacks in supple fingers, threw balls all the way to the clouds. *I hated them!* All of them, every one of them! I hated their strong legs that matched. I hated their muscles that thoughtlessly and faultlessly obeyed their commands. I hated their easy activity, when I was condemned to spend the rest of my life dragging my useless leg around like a badge of dishonor given me by that pig of a drunken driver who had crushed it, and with it my very life, when I was only five years old."

"You were once a child? I thought you simulacra were—."

"Merely a manner of speaking. I remember what it was like and that is almost the same thing. But you were talking about dancing, as I recall."

"Yes. Everyone seems so contented. They don't seem to mind that they are—are—."

"Cripples."

"Yes."

"They have come out of the shadows and from behind drawn shades. They have entered life. They have come here to the Valley, where blindness doesn't stop one from wearing gloriously brocaded silk even though one cannot see the cloth for oneself. Others can see it, and they tell the sightless one how beautiful it is and that is sufficient. The sound of the metal tips on the pegs of all the wooden legs make a very modern music which is a joy to hear once one's ears have become accustomed to it. The deaf—that old man there, for example—notice how he follows the movements of those whose ears hear. He can see the brocades, and that is a pleasure. So he does not mind so much that he cannot hear the music. All of us have our compensations."

"They are all simulacra."

"Of course."

"Where did they come from?"

"They were made."

"You made them?"

"They were made for me so that my world would

make a kind of sense I could stand. Just as Super-stud's women were made for him.''

"Are they—,'' Smith pointed to the dancers, "—happy here? Are you?''

"How could we not be?'' Crutch countered. "Here no one mocks us. Here, although those of us without legs hobble, there is no one to watch us with pity in their eyes. The blind see vistas more beautiful than sighted eyes can detect, and no one here ridicules such seers' visions. Yes, we are all happy here. Perhaps you will learn how to be happy here also.''

A girl twirled from the center of the crowd to its shifting fringe. And stopped. She stood quite still for a moment, her arms awry, her legs and lips parted, caught like an image in a slow-motion summer day, transfixed.

Smith, attracted by her beauty that was softly gossamering the air about them both, took a step toward her as if drawn by some force soundless but insistent. She turned her head slowly so that her sightless eyes rested upon him. Then, slightly shifting the position of her head as does one who listens carefully, she began to move toward him, her hands reaching out, her hair flowing out behind her as if it too danced to the music of the cymbals.

"Hello,'' she said when she stood in front of Smith. "My name is Iris.''

"Mine is Smith. Hello.'' He stared into her eyes and thought he saw colors there that he had never seen before. But a more careful inspection revealed that her eyes were an ordinary blue.

As her hands rose and came to rest on his cheeks, Smith smiled gently, aware that she could not see his smile but sensing that she would nevertheless know that it was there upon his face.

She said, "The bones of your face, they are as fine as china and yet as strong as crowns." Her cool fingers played over his features. She touched his nose as water touches the rocks over which it flows. She ran the tips of her fingers along the curved flesh of his ears and lipline. She investigated his forehead and traced the lines of his brows and lashes that arched over and under his eyes. "Your hair," she murmured. "It is as long as mine. It is white but not in the way of snow. No, it is white as egrets are white and as lovely. Your skin, how bronzed with the sun it is!"

"My hair is black," Smith said. "My skin is pale."

She ignored his contradictions. She took his hands in hers. "You are a gardener. One who works in houses that are hot where orchids grow. I see," she continued, taking a step backward, "that you are a prince who will one day reign over roses with a benign and understanding gentility."

"Iris is blind," Crutch interposed, "as you can observe. She sees splendors sighted persons miss. Ugliness makes itself known to her in secret ways."

"Iris is so beautiful," Smith said, "that she blinds me."

Iris' laughter joined the music to make it even more joyous. "Will you dance with me, Smith?"

He glanced hesitantly at Crutch, who waved him forward, urging him to follow Iris. She was already moving back toward the throng of revelers in their wheeled chairs and crippled gaiety.

"Take care!" Smith cried as Iris stumbled against a stone in her path.

"It is a ship," she called back to him, touching the stone tenderly with one bare foot. "It sails on seas of grass and ground. If I had the time, I would board it and visit shores where the sand is made of sweet salt and the trees bear diamonds instead of oranges. But now there are other things to do, important things. Smith?"

"Here," he said and touched her hand.

"You are not here," she told him as their bodies bent in time to the music and their four feet explored the terrain that supported them. "Where are you, Smith?"

Her comment and her question caused the anxiety to shiver through him once again. Blind though she was, she saw clearly. He found himself wishing for her kind of sight, sight that would let him visualize diamond-bearing trees and understand why a man's memory had been stolen, turning him into someone he did not know.

"Where have you lost yourself?" Iris asked him.

The music grew louder around them. Drums grumbled. Chimes cheered.

"I like to dance," he said, realizing it was so.

"Do *you*? Or does the man you are becoming?"

"Listen to the music."

"Hold me closer."

Smith obeyed and was surprised to find that he too could see the diamonds sparkling in the dry climate that nourished the strange trees Iris had spoken about. "I did not know that cripples danced."

"You did not know? How odd! Then you probably do not know that many men with strong legs never dance. Did you know that?"

"Yes, I knew." Smith realized with some amazement that, yes, he did know.

"I can see," Iris said, her voice low, "that your

strong legs move, but minus their proper music. I see too that your feet would avoid crushing insects as they move to their own small music."

"No, that's not true." Visions of crushed and bleeding insects crossed Smith's mind. Insects? Broken bodies, torn limbs. Insects?

"I am talking about the man you are becoming," Iris explained in response to his protest. "Not about the man you once were."

"That man—."

"He is dead. I can see him sleeping. His dreams were webs woven by deadly spiders. But you are a phoenix. His fire gave you birth, but you may one day choose to renounce its flames."

Smith said nothing more as he and Iris continued their dance amid the others who now completely surrounded them. As Iris placed her cheek against his shoulder, Smith watched the faces of the other dancers. He marveled at the pleasure he found there and marveled too at the dexterity with which even the most deformed danced their private minuets and improvised waltzes. As he watched, he became aware of a naked girl moving uneasily among the dancers as if she were in the company of strangers whose behavior confused her. She did not dance. She walked as sleepers walk when still trapped in the depths of their dreams. She moved awkwardly, although her slender body suggested the possibility of a more graceful carriage. Her feet barely lifted from the ground as she turned first one way and then the other in her effort to avoid colliding with those near her. She wasn't beautiful, Smith decided, remembering the girls summoned by Superstud's computer. They had made him think of night and night's dark rites. This girl—this woman—made him think of mornings when the sun returns rich with promise and fat with warmth to the world it had temporarily abandoned.

The girl was close to him now, and without fully realizing what he was doing, he released his hold on Iris and began to walk toward her. The closer he came to her, the more a mercurial memory slid through his mind, a memory he could not identify in the confusion of his thoughts, but one, he was convinced, that related in some way to the girl who now stood motionless ahead of him as if she were waiting for someone.

"Smith?" Iris called out, her empty eyes unblinking. As if he had answered her, she added, "Yes, human beings must go where they must go. Crutch told me so." Then she turned away from him and let herself be taken in the handless arms of a man whose face was wet with tears while he laughed and bounced her and himself about to the dull mutter of the drums and the fluttering notes of the flutes.

When Smith reached the girl, he took her hand. The instant he did so, he knew she was different from Iris and from Crutch and from all the others who inhabited the Valley of the Maimed.

She shook herself free of his grip. She studied his face as she stood stiffly in front of him.

Smith wondered if she was seeing what Iris had seen when she had looked at his face with the help of her sensitive hands and fingers. Was this girl seeing a prince who would reign over roses? A man whose feet could not crush insects?

"You don't belong here," he said to her.

After a moment, "No, I don't."

"Neither do I. Not now."

"Not now?"

"Not now that I've met you. You're not like the others here. You're like me."

"I am not a machine," she said harshly.

"Nor am I."

She stared at him for a moment, examining his face and then letting her gaze wander skeptically down the length of his body. She reached out and her hands crept behind the soft flesh of his ear lobes.

As she withdrew her hands, Smith said, "Perhaps you believe me now. I'm not a simulacrum. I'm as human as you are." He was certain that she too was human. He felt no need to try to detect any wheels or dials on her body. There was a light in her eyes that could not be manufactured. It alone made such an investigation unnecessary. There was, too, a natural texture to her skin which in no way resembled the unnaturally stiff covering that was common to the simulacra.

Crutch came up to them. "There are two of you now. Both of you are welcome to remain here."

The girl began to shake her head, her eyes on Smith.

"What is your name?" Crutch asked her.

"Rachel," she answered. "I can remember my first name—but nothing else. Everything else is so confused in my mind." She asked Smith, "Who are you?"

Feeling a shame for which he could not account, Smith replied, "I call myself Smith."

Suddenly, a male simulacrum sidled up to them, its eyes on emptiness, its mouth twisted into a pink and tortured snake. He screamed. A giggle followed his scream.

Rachel took a tentative step in Smith's direction.

A second scream sounded, curiously lacking the sharp edge of agony.

Crutch said, "You see and hear the visible manifestations of the damage done to him."

Smith put his arm around Rachel's waist.

"There are imps loose within his skull," Crutch explained. "They torment one another and him as well. That is why he is here in the Valley."

The simulacrum began to hop up and down, muttering, salivating.

"He dances," Crutch said, "to his own music, which none of the rest of us can hear. Does he trouble you?"

Rachel nodded, her face not so much fearful as concerned.

The simulacrum ceased its hopping and began to rip his clothes to shreds. "I am a man," he muttered savagely. "So I feed on private angers and drink a brew of hate. Love is not in me nor is pity. Come with me and I will show you where worms feed on dead flesh, flesh that once housed dreams before it grew old and the harpy Truth came to ride its back and flay its buttocks. You talk to me of peace? Of the intricate ways I differ from other apes? Mere words! Mere thistles blown away by a bitter wind. Aging fireflies whose lights grow dim. Come with me and I will reveal to you—reveal to you—reveal—."

Crutch struck the simulacrum a light blow on the shoulder.

There was a shuddering, a faint clicking from somewhere within his clawed and self-mutilated body, and then, "—reveal to you how I was born hungering, lived a tapestry of grievous lies and will die with no nobility, like a decrepit beast who knows that it helped to create and sustain the uncaring jungle which will witness its hopeless death."

The simulacrum began to back away from them, his head jerking and his index finger beckoning, an obscene expression on his ruined face.

Rachel turned her face away. Smith watched him until he disappeared among his no longer dancing companions, who were now laying out a picnic on the grass.

He was about to turn back to Rachel to ask the questions that had begun to bubble up within him when blue fire streaked up from the midst of the picnicking simularcra. A second streak of color seared the sky—red.

"What is it?" Rachel cried.

"Fireworks," Crutch answered. "The one you just met, the mad one, he is determined to blind the sun so that it will not be forced to look upon what has taken place in our world."

"What has taken place?" Smith demanded.

"Stop it!" Crutch cried to the maddened figure in the crowd, as his efforts made more fires soar into the sky. "If you don't stop it—!"

Crutch spun around at the blast of sound in the distance. He gazed up at the top of the hill where Marsman, a convoluted horn to his lips, blew blunt and alarming noises, causing the Valley below him to echo brassily.

"Run!" a female simulacrum screamed from the center of the crowd, dropping her white linen cloth and gathering up her skirts.

"It is war!" boomed Marsman from his hilltop. "I see it declared there in the sky!"

"No!" Crutch shouted. "It was only fireworks!"

Marsman whirled his horn about his head and then brought it to his lips.

Its blasts sent the simulacra into a panic of unplanned flight. They ran, those who had legs. They wheeled, those trapped in their chairs.

The mad simulacrum paid them no attention, entranced as he was by the many matches he was lighting and by the sky above him which was laced with spectral fire.

"Marsman!" Crutch cried in desperation. "We will defend ourselves! We have metal trusses with which to strike deadly blows. Our splints can crack skulls. *Marsman*—!"

The last word of Crutch's plea vanished in the avalanche of sound caused by Marsman's horse galloping ridered down the breast of the hill. Above Marsman, strange figures appeared on the hilltop as if sprouting from it, and then they too came tumbling down behind their roaring leader who was brandishing his feathered lance and laughing out loud.

"Skeletons!" Smith exclaimed, watching Marsman's army advance.

"Of course. Only the dead love death," Crutch cried. "The living have happier paramours. *Flee!*"

"Smith!" Rachel cried, her eyes bright with terror as she looked about her in search of some sanctuary.

"This way!" Smith responded, seizing her wrist and running toward one of the distant caverns that gaped in the side of the opposite slope.

Under the sky's womb, in which the mad simulacrum's fire still glowed, and not far from the hooves of Marsman's horse, they ran. Simulacra traced geometric designs as they crossed and recrossed their path in their disjointed flight from the one who sought to steal what was left of their lives.

Behind them all, Marsman signaled to his soldiers, and the phalanx of clattering bones divided neatly into three groups. The group in the center remained behind Marsman, riding hard and sweatless down toward the heart of the Valley. The other two sections rode outward in a flanking movement. Within minutes, the flankers had cut off the escape of the fleeing simulacra. They herded them back toward the center of the Valley, where Marsman and his contingent of white warriors were headed.

"Death!" bellowed Marsman, raising his arm.

With a brittle resonance, the skeletons massed on three sides of the trapped simulacra, armored safely in their lifelessness, with raised spears and lances.

Marsman brought his arm down.

Up went the spears and lances to slice the air and then down they came to pierce already blinded eyes, to sever more segments from already maimed limbs, to finally halt the *thrumming* in alarmed and artificial breasts.

Rachel, running, looked back and moaned.

Smith gripped her wrist more tightly and on they ran, the mouth of the cavern growing wider as they neared it.

Oil spurted from the falling bodies of the stricken simulacra. Grease that had once limbered their arms and legs oozed. Released from their manufactured prisons, springs uncoiled to *twing* upward and then sprawl their metal circularity on the ground.

The attack continued. Crutch raised his wooden weapon and struck the skeleton nearest him, sending it careening to the ground.

A few of the still functioning simulacra fought back with the steel claws that had replaced their hands. Others flung their canes at the skeletons. One woman fiercely stabbed a horse with the sharp steel edge of her body brace, causing its awful white rider to fall and lie still.

Smith and Rachel had reached the mouth of the cavern when they suddenly found themselves cut off from their sought haven by a towering skeleton on a gaunt horse.

Rachel clung to Smith, her breathing audible, sweat shining on her tense face.

"Kill!" shouted Marsman in the noisy distance.

The skeleton's sword quivered in its hand, and Smith sprang forward to seize it. As he did so, its tip touched his upper arm. Tearing cloth and flesh, it opened a four-inch-long wound, a fleshy chasm from which his blood flowed freely.

Marsman suddenly shouted a command to the skeleton, which sheathed its sword, turned its horse, and rode off. Marsman galloped across the littered Valley and reined his horse sharply when he arrived beside Smith and Rachel.

"Blood," he said, looking down at the redness staining Smith's arm.

Smith said nothing as Rachel stepped behind him.

"You really are—," Marsman began.

"I am human," Smith snapped angrily. "But does that matter to you?"

Marsman's face darkened as he stared down at Smith. Idly, he ran his thick fingers along the skull tied to his belt. "Of what use are humans?" he asked, more of himself than of Smith, and then he answered his own question. "They can fight. I remember that.

And you—there is something about you, Smith. Something that appeals to me. I am not a man to whom much appeals but—."

"You are not a man," Smith reminded him.

"But I live because of men," Marsman shot back. "I am made in their image." He hesitated and then pointed at Rachel. "Who is your woman?"

"Rachel is her name."

"I will kill her, and then you and I—."

"Rachel is human too," Smith said quickly.

"Ah! I have never known a human woman. The women I have taken have all been simulacra. Perhaps she need not die."

"Smith," Rachel whispered. "What will he—?"

Marsman's laughter shattered the quiet of the Valley, now a gigantic graveyard. "What will I do to you, Rachel?" He waited a moment, and then leaning down, he seized her waist and in one swift, easy movement, lifted her up to share his saddle with him.

"Wait!" Smith yelled, but Marsman jerked the reins and his horse reared wildly and sped off, trampling the already ruined bodies of the simulacra beneath its thoughtless hooves.

"Wait!" Smith yelled a second time as Rachel called his name, her voice a wail on the windless air. A devastating sense of loss swept over him as he began to run rapidly, not after Marsman but after the woman named Rachel who had stirred something within him, something he knew he needed to end his terrible aloneness.

Marsman raced up the side of the hill, his army of silent skeletons accompanying him.

Smith ran through the Valley and was about to ascend the hill when he saw Crutch kneeling on the

ground, his head in his hands, his tears for the now
hopelessly maimed and crippled falling on unconcerned ground.

Smith halted and stood in silence for a moment
above Crutch. "I'm sorry," he said finally.

Crutch looked up at him, his green eyes melting.
"Sorry? For what? For whom? For these?" He waved
his crutch as if it were a wand over the shattered steel
and escaped lubricants.

"No," Smith said softly. "I'm sorry for you."

"Why?" The single word whipped out of Crutch's
mouth and struck Smith.

"Because now you will be noticed. People like me
will no longer see your face or hear your words. They
will see only your injured leg and hear only the
rhythm of your odd walk."

Crutch lowered his head. He reached out to gently
touch the body of one of the destroyed simulacra.
"What am I to do now? Where can I go?"

"I'm sorry," Smith repeated.

When Crutch did not respond, he turned and resumed his pursuit of Rachel, knowing there was
nothing he could do to help either Crutch or his companions. He tore strips of cloth free from his shirt
and bound his wounded arm. When he finally
reached the crest of the hill, he stumbled and fell.

A moment later, when his vision, momentarily
blurred, had cleared, he saw that Marsman was waiting for him on the other side of the hill. The skeletons had vanished.

"I have recruited a warrior and a wife in one short
battle," Marsman shouted up to him. "Come, soldier!"

Smith got to his feet and walked down the hill, his

eyes on Rachel as he tried to think of how he could prevent the mating Marsman obviously had in mind.

"Will you serve me?" Marsman asked as Smith approached him. "Or will you die?" He raised his lance.

"I will serve you," Smith replied, already planning to terminate his service by slaughtering the murderous simulacrum who would be his master.

Chapter 4

"THE OATH," Marsman declared as Smith arrived to stand beside the blood-red horse that was tossing its huge head in the air. "The warrior's oath. You must swear it. Repeat after me, I, Smith—."

"I, Smith—."

"Do bloodily swear—."

"Do bloodily swear—." Smith's eyes met Rachel's.

"To destroy the enemy, possess his women, enslave his offspring even as I am now enslaved by the mighty Marsman."

Smith repeated the ugly words in a neutral voice that gave no hint of the fury he was feeling as he gazed at Marsman's leather-encased legs tightly spanning his horse's heaving ribs. He avoided the sight of Marsman's groin where it was pressed tightly against Rachel's naked buttocks as she sat in front of him upon the heavy saddle. His mouth had become dry, and the blood in his veins seemed to have stilled ominously.

Marsman took the coiled rope that hung from his saddle horn and created a hangman's noose at one end of it. He dropped the noose over Smith's head, tightened it, and wound the other end around the saddle horn.

Smith lurched forward as Marsman spurred his horse and began to move off into the shadows spilling from the descending evening. Recovering his balance, he found himself forced to trot at a brisk pace to keep the rope from growing too taut and strangling him.

They traveled for some time, night replaced evening and stars lighted the sky above them. Just when Smith felt certain he could run no more behind his captor's snorting stallion, Marsman drew on the reins, and they halted.

"My fortress," Marsman declared, pointing.

Smith stared into the gloom. Some thirty yards distant was a tall, solidly built structure of stones that he recognized as having been taken from the fields and hills in the surrounding area. From the four corners of the fortress torches flared suddenly as if in welcome. Somewhere an animal bellowed. Smith was not sure whether the sound came from within or from without the fortress.

"It is here that I plan my campaigns," Marsman announced. "It is here that I lie awake at night and dream of an orgy of pain in which my enemy suffers greatly before pleading with me to present him with the ultimate gift—death."

"Who is your enemy, Marsman?" Smith asked.

The simulacrum turned slightly in his saddle to stare down at his captive. "He is everywhere. He is Evil."

"But how do you recognize him?"

"Come inside," Marsman directed. He spoke in a pleasant tone, as if Smith and Rachel had a choice. But the rope around Smith's neck lent the lie to choice as did Marsman's strong arm that was clasped tightly around Rachel's waist.

Marsman dismounted and stood before the iron door set in the stone walls. It swung open to admit him. He led his horse through the open area just inside the gate and finally halted in front of a rude hut. He pulled Rachel down from his horse and held her with one hand while clutching the rope that linked him to Smith. He strode forward and entered the hut, his prisoners following him.

When he dropped the rope, Smith said, "I asked you a question. How do you recognize your enemy? Do the stars reveal him to you? Does he wear a brand on his forehead?"

"I know him," Marsman answered emphatically. "I know him because he is unlike me and would do me harm. He would shatter the cities I love and raze the sanctuaries where I sometimes take refuge. I know him because he does not look like me nor does he walk or talk like me. I need no star to guide me to him. I can find him locked in any midnight or roaming about among multitudes."

"Can you find friends as easily as foes?"

Marsman glared at Smith. "I have no friends."

"Why is that?"

"Because friends encumber one. They keep me from my task."

"Which is?"

"To seek out and then destroy my enemy. I am a dedicated man, Smith. My concubines are duty, loyalty, courage. Demanding wenches all."

As Smith listened to Marsman speak of his life and how he lived it, he became aware of a feeling of sympathy for the simulacrum. But that sympathy was misplaced he decided, as he recalled the skeletons under Marsman's command and how they had moved among the inhabitants of the Valley of the Maimed, reaping their gruesome harvest. He could not account for his softened feeling. It was certainly not generated by Marsman's appearance. The skull tied emblematically to his thick belt was repellent as both reality and symbol. The simulacrum's face, so pale an oasis around the jet pools of his eyes, was a testament to a dark yearning that Smith found appalling. And yet his feeling of sympathy persisted. At times, as Marsman spoke, he thought he heard an echo of another voice, one faintly familiar, one that he suspected was only a product of his own imagination. Still, he found himself contemplating the service to which he had committed himself and discovered that he no longer found it quite as abhorrent as he had at first thought it. Nor did his plan to destroy Marsman seem quite as sharp-edged now as it had at first. Could it be, he asked himself, watching Marsman pace briskly back and forth in front of him, that I pity this creature?

"War is the crucible in which men are truly tested," Marsman thundered before Smith had an opportunity to frame an answer to the question he had just posed for himself. "It is the arena in which heroes are born. But I grow tired of talking. Talking is for women whose sinews are weak and who have only their tongues to use as weapons. Stand there, Smith." Marsman pointed to a section of the hut's floor that was ringed by a deep trough. He pointed to a similar area next to it. "You, woman—stand there."

Smith obeyed. So did Rachel.

Marsman did something secretive with his fingers —Smith thought he heard them snap—and the result was a burst of tall flame that snaked out into the trough surrounding the area in which Smith stood. Marsman repeated his ritual and fire also circled Rachel.

"Prisoners," Marsman declared coldly, "dream always of escape. Thus, this fire." He walked to the wall opposite the prisons he had just created and touched a button protruding from it.

Rachel, startled, cried out as an odorous liquid poured down upon her and simultaneously upon Smith.

"Gasoline," Marsman informed them. "Now, should either of you so much as touch a single finger to the flames surrounding you, you will turn into torches. I go now to consult with colonels, to talk tactics with those who know that war is sacred and cowardice the only sin. Smith, think of battles and how they may be won. Rachel, spend your time imagining my needs, which you must devise clever ways of satisfying."

He tightened his belt about his waist and stalked toward the door.

When he had gone, Smith stood on tiptoe so that he could catch glimpses of Rachel between the walls of fire that separated them from one another. "Don't be afraid," he advised her.

"I am afraid."

"There's enough room within the circle so that you won't be burned."

"It's not the fire that frightens me."

Smith hesitated as a question sprang to his lips. A part of him did not want to ask it. Nevertheless, "What frightens you?"

Rachel, her arms wrapped about her body that was rosied by the light of the fire, said nothing for a moment. She turned her head from side to side as if she were examining the peripheries of her prison. "Smith," she said finally, "I don't know who I am."

"You're Rachel," he offered lamely.

"Yes, I'm sure that's my first name. But what about the rest? What is my last name? Where are we?"

For a time, concepts scattered in Smith's brain. Before and after. Then and now. But time, to be meaningful, needed a point of reference. His referent seemed to have been lost just as Rachel's had been. What of his life before he had awakened in the unfamiliar casket?

"Rachel," he began, "when I found you in the Valley—where had you come from?"

"There was an enormous hall—or maybe it was some kind of auditorium," she replied. "I awoke there—in a glass box. I climbed out of it and wandered out of the building. Eventually, I came to the Valley."

"I also awoke in the hall you just mentioned," he told her, delighted to find that they shared at least a brief history involving a mysterious sleep and an equally mysterious awakening. "Before you went to sleep—. Rachel, can you remember anything about that time?"

The flames springing up around both of them seemed to lower as if they were awaiting her answer. When she spoke, they leaped higher in the air and for a moment Smith thought their tongues might touch the ceiling.

"No. Not being able to remember anything makes me feel so lost."

Rachel's reply caused Smith to feel drawn to her by more than her simple beauty or the faint prodding of barely disguised lust that arose in him as he caught glimpses of her naked body. They were both victims of the same unknown force. He was glad that the same sense of loss he had been feeling was shared by someone else.

"Smith."

"Yes?"

"I wish Marsman had imprisoned us together."

"No fire burns forever," he told her after a moment's hesitation. "We'll be together, you and I."

"I sometimes think we were together."

"Yes, we were. In the Valley."

"No. Not just there. Somewhere else. In another time." She drew back the hair that slanted down on both sides of her face.

"I know you now!" Smith shouted above the sound of the flames. "I saw you in the hall. There was another woman there too—but I remember you. I disconnected the cable that was attached to your forehead. Sleeping, you looked like you do now with your hair drawn back."

"Who are we, Smith?"

"We're human beings. It is a beginning, that knowledge."

"And you believe that one day you and I will be together."

"Yes," Smith said firmly, "I do."

"Then perhaps we can bear whatever else may happen in the meantime."

"We'll survive."

"That may not be enough," Rachel said quickly. "To survive is one thing. To live is something else."

Smith remained silent.

Rachel spoke again, some time later. "Smith, you don't hate Marsman, do you?"

Her question surprised him. He considered it.

"No, I don't."

"I watched you while he was here before. You looked sorrowful."

"I don't hate Marsman," Smith said. "I do feel sorry for him. To be in love with death as he is is a sad thing."

"At times, I thought you were like him. And yet you do not look at all like him."

"I wonder who made him," Smith speculated.

"I wonder why he was made."

"The other humans like us—they sleep while the simulacra make war and love."

"Love?" Rachel frowned.

Smith told her about Superstud and his computerized harem. He was pleased to hear the faint sound of her laughter filtering across to him through the flames as he described Superstud's obsession.

When her laughter ended, she said, "There are so many questions and so few answers."

"You must be tired," he said, not wanting to be reminded of the truth of what she had just said because of the unease it engendered within him. "Try to sleep." He watched as she stretched and then, after giving him a weak smile, sank from his sight behind the fire encircling her.

He stood for a time and stared into the flames that hid Rachel from him. But soon their heavy heat combined with his own fatigue to overwhelm him. He lay down wearily on the hard floor of his prison and was almost instantly asleep. The twisted dreams that came to him told him no translatable truth about the man he once had been.

His dreams ended abruptly some unknown amount of time later as the sound of singing invaded the hut. He awoke and rose to his feet. It took him several seconds to realize that the flames no longer flared around him. At the same time, he recognized Marsman moving about in the hut's dim interior, his raucous voice rising and falling as the words of his battle hymn racketed tunelessly off the walls.

"Rachel!" Smith exclaimed as he discovered that she was gone from the room.

"*Rachel! Rachel!*" Marsman mocked, his voice trembling with false nervousness. "Never mind the woman, Smith. On your feet and mettle as well. This day awaits us in which glory will be ours."

"Where is Rachel?" Smith demanded, striding across the room. When he reached Marsman, he seized the simulacrum's shoulder to spin him around, but Marsman kicked his foot back viciously and sent Smith sprawling on the floor in the center of the room.

He turned quickly and placed one booted foot on Smith's chest. Although Smith seized it with both hands, he could not remove it.

Marsman stared down at him, no expression on his face. "It might serve me better should I send my lance exploring beneath that thin skin of yours, Smith. And yet, I am a patient—even a tolerant man. I will let you live and have your chance to die nobly and with grace in the contest facing us this day. I will so do, I say, only if you show me that you possess the sly wisdom of the enslaved."

Smith squirmed beneath Marsman's foot but he could not escape it. "Where's Rachel?"

"I have ordered that she be taken to join our other camp followers. The men who took her have been told to slay her at the first sign of your disobedience, to strike her mightily at your first display of impudence. I am gambling, I know. But warriors must always gamble. It is their profession. I believe you will not act in a way that will bring her harm. Am I a shrewd gambler, Smith?"

"Let me up!"

Instead of complying with the request, Marsman pressed his foot harder against Smith's chest. "Answer me!"

"You are a shrewd gambler," Smith managed to gasp as Marsman forced the air from his lungs.

"I do believe it. Still, it is good to hear you confirm it." Marsman casually withdrew his foot. Smith started to rise but Marsman held up a hand. "Slaves belong on their knees, a fitting position from which they render obeisance to those they serve. Stay so!"

Smith, kneeling, wanted nothing more than to spring to his feet and attack Marsman. He fought this urge by summoning a bright image of Rachel's face to his mind. He did not doubt Marsman's description of the orders he had given concerning her. He could not therefore obey his impulse—not now and not yet. But he had learned that situations changed. He would wait for an auspicious time and then he would . . .

"Use this on these," Marsman ordered, handing Smith a wooden bowl and pointing to the black leather boots he wore which reached halfway up his thick thighs.

Smith took the bowl containing a partially congealed substance. He looked about him for something he could use to apply it to the boots looming in front of his face as Marsman, hands on lean hips, stood haughtily above him, waiting.

"Your fingers are strong and supple, Smith. Use them!"

Smith hesitated briefly, wanting more than anything else in his strange world at that instant to fling the wooden bowl into the proud face that gazed down upon him, waiting to witness his humiliation. He bent his head and, holding the bowl in his left hand, thrust the four fingers of his right hand into the substance it contained. He applied it to the toes of Marsman's boots, spreading it thinly.

"Rub it in!" Marsman barked. "Massage the leather so that it flexes readily."

Smith rubbed harder, and when he had used the entire contents of the bowl on Marsman's boots, the simulacrum ordered him to continue his manipulation of the leather that was growing supple beneath his fingers.

Smith obeyed, heat blossoming in his fingertips from the friction as he rubbed briskly, working the substance fully into the leather.

"Neither water nor blood will invade them now," Marsman declared with pleasure as he slapped his hands against the tops of both boots. "Now they are practical as well as beautiful. See how brightly you have made them shine, Smith. Except there—in that single spot." He pointed.

Smith bent again and rubbed the dull spot until it too gleamed.

"Now," Marsman declared when he was finally satisfied with Smith's efforts, "we must gird ourselves. Come with me!"

He led the way to a draped alcove and uncovered it with a single sweep of his long arm. "Armor," he announced, pointing. "Weapons." He selected a mailed and hooded garment made in a single, shroud-like piece. He took from a shelf a curved blade with a metal handle and then chose a broad belt from which to hang it. A helmet next, with a thick visor.

He tossed all the items he had removed from the alcove to the floor at Smith's feet and then, pulling off his boots first, proceeded to disrobe. When he stood naked before Smith, he made an abrupt gesture.

Smith obeyed the wordless signal. Silently, he helped Marsman dress himself in his chosen martial garments.

"Here," Marsman said when he was no longer naked. He flung similar clothing at Smith and waited while he dressed himself in them.

Marsman appraised him carefully. He stepped forward and drew the belt Smith wore a notch tighter. He jerked it downward, saying as he did so that a belt and the curved sword that hung from it should hang neatly on the hips to allow the torso to swivel readily to avoid or, preferably, to deliver blows. Then he reached into the dim interior of the alcove and drew out a heavy mirror which he promptly held up to Smith.

Smith was genuinely startled by the image of himself trapped in the mirror Marsman was holding up to him. He wore a thick suit of mail that covered his entire body and fitted him surprisingly well. His head was covered with a helmet not unlike the one Marsman wore. A doublet of bright blue cloth hung from his shoulders, a gay addition to the somber chain mail that hid his flesh. Spikes protruded from his gloved knuckles as they did from the mail covering his knees.

"Come!" Marsman commanded, dropping the mirror.

Smith followed him outside and found a skeleton standing at the entrance holding the reins which drooped from the bridles of two horses. He immediately recognized Marsman's red horse. The other one was black.

"Yours," said Marsman, indicating the black horse. He mounted his own animal.

The skeleton tossed the remaining set of reins to Smith who, imitating Marsman's movements, placed one foot in a stirrup and swung himself up into the saddle. He was surprised at the ease with which he had performed the action. Some kinesthetic sense had guided him, although he could not recall ever having sat in a saddle before.

Marsman raised his arm and his horse moved forward. Smith, without conscious thought, kicked his heels against the flanks of his own mount and was soon abreast of Marsman. Behind them came the skeletons, their advance a grim symphony of grinding bones.

"Where are we going?" Smith asked above the noise Marsman's soldiers could not help making.

"To war," Marsman replied. "Ride six paces behind me as befits your station," he ordered Smith. "The only time you may ride abreast of me or in front of me is when dust billows down from the hills so that you might deflect it from me."

Smith reined his horse and fell back behind Marsman. They passed through the iron gate and out into the world beyond Marsman's fortress. Smith turned to look back at it, thinking of Rachel. He was delighted to see her in the midst of a group of women who were riding donkeys out through the still open gate. He would have turned his horse and ridden back to greet her, risking his master's wrath, but the skeletons ranged behind him presented an impenetrable barrier. Through the spaces between their bones,

70

he watched Rachel and the other women urging their donkeys onward, two tall skeletons shepherding them as the prodded some of the more languid beasts.

Rachel wore a loose gray gown bound tightly at her throat. Its long sleeves hid her arms, revealing only her hands. Her feet were bare and her face was set in an expression that Smith correctly interpreted as resignation.

"Rachel!" he shouted.

Her head rose in response to his cry, and when she saw him her body straightened. She called his name in return, her face brightening, her expression of resignation changing to one of recognition tinged with hope.

"Marsman!" Smith yelled, spurring his horse forward but careful to remain the prescribed six paces behind the simulacrum. "Why are the women following us?"

"Women always follow their men in time of war. It is a tradition made holy by experience and blessed by custom. But this time, there is a purpose to their presence more important than the services they are accustomed to providing when long marches end and soldiers seek surcease from their weariness."

"What is it, this purpose you speak of?"

"They will bear witness to the deed we will do. It will chasten their tempers and make humble and mild their natures."

"The deed you say we will do, what is it?"

Marsman did not respond immediately, as his horse began to mount a hill that seemed familiar to Smith.

Smith repeated his question, more loudly this time.

"We go to engage the enemy," Marsman replied.

"That's no answer. It tells me nothing."

"Down there!" Marsman shouted back to Smith as they reached the crest of the hill.

Smith looked in the direction Marsman was pointing and saw only trees and bushes, a riotous growth of grass and unkempt hedges.

Marsman turned, noticing Smith's frown, and amplified his explanation. "Look there to the south. Do you not see that ancient tree that leans as if it were about to fall? Now do you see our enemy?"

Smith examined the tree Marsman had identified and found an untreelike growth that, in the light of the rising sun, seemed to him to be a part of it. But then he became aware of what it was that he was actually seeing. The strange growth was not part of the tree to which Marsman had pointed. It was made of metal. It was, he realized, a part of Superstud's computer. His realization brought him only further confusion. The computer was their enemy? He had already begun to suspect Marsman of madness. Perhaps now his suspicions were about to mature into facts.

"It should be an easy victory," he observed, careful to dull the edge of sarcasm in his tone. "That computer is unarmed, and we are many and weaponed."

Marsman snorted. "The computer is not our enemy, fool! I am not interested at this time in destroying the tree. I want only to chastise its fruit."

"Superstud's girls!" Smith exclaimed as understanding swept over him.

"Precisely. The women behind us have of late nurtured dangerous notions that I cannot in conscientious chauvinism endorse. They speak among themselves of rights and respect. From such talk, revolution grows. I have therefore decided to render such insolent talk powerless. We will summon Superstud's whores and make of them examples from which our women shall learn much."

Before Smith could express the sense of alarm he felt, Marsman was riding down the hillside toward the computer. Smith, because of the puppet-like responsiveness of the skeletons behind him, had no choice but to gallop after the one who was, for a time at least, his master.

Marsman's horse skidded to a turf-tearing halt in front of the bland face of the computer. He sprang from his saddle and, confronting the computer, pounded angrily on its glass face.

No crack appeared in the glass.

He kicked the machine.

Nothing happened.

"The buttons," Smith volunteered as he rode up behind Marsman. "If I remember correctly, you're supposed to push the buttons and when you do, the girls will appear. You can see that all the buttons are labeled. That one just above your shoulder there, for example—it says, D-Cup. And the one next to it: 44, 28, 32."

Marsman gave Smith a stony glance. "I didn't come here to enjoy. I came to chastise. I told you that!"

Smith shrugged his shoulders.

The skeletons were busily herding Rachel and the other women to one side. Another contingent of Marsman's white warriors were setting up prefabricated plastic bleachers for them to sit on.

"What are you smirking for?" Marsman roared at Smith. "Slaves are not allowed to smirk. Get down at once and summon the wenches."

Smith dismounted and approached the computer. "What did you have in mind, Marsman?"

"Girls!"

"Aha! I suspected it!"

The simulacrum's pale face grew paler. "That is not what I meant! I meant that I want them summoned—for suitable and educational instruction."

Smith gave Marsman a slight bow that was in no way obsequious, and then he stepped up to the computer and pressed a series of buttons.

A humming. Clicks.

Girls. Peacocking up to Marsman, simpering seductively.

"The Book!" Marsman called out.

One of the skeletons clattered up to him with a Bible, which he grabbed and began to use to fend off the eager females.

Smith edged away and found a seat next to Rachel on the bleachers. "Hello," he whispered.

"What is Marsman going to do?" she whispered.

"Watch," he ordered, smiling.

"—and you make of yourselves Man's enemy!" Marsman was intoning, his face solemn, the Bible pressed tightly against his stomach and slowly sliding downward. "Loose of tongue and morals be you all so that a man suffers emasculation on the one hand and fatigue on the other. Reform and repent, I command you. Armageddon awaits you if you do else. The Four Horsemen are riding this way, the spoor of your sins a stench in their nostrils!"

The girls stood still, obviously impressed and somewhat disconcerted by Marsman's words, which he had uttered with ferocity and priestly enthusiasm. As he rambled on about how women should abstain from criticizing their mates and embrace humility in the home and modesty in the presence of members of the opposite sex, the girls dropped their eyes and nervously drew the loose folds of their few garments about themselves.

"If you must talk of liberation," Marsman told them, the Bible still anchored in its restless and secretly aroused harbor, "then let it be in fitting terms of liberation from too much independence, which only muddies the female mind and adds spicy fevers to already overheated female blood. Cast down your eyes in the presence of men! Think lovingly of children and abandon chastity only when your mate comes careening to your chamber in a wild humor. Only at such a time should you indulge the evil that is both your nature and Man's enemy!"

A girl with skin the color of bumblebees began to weep. As if her lamentations were a signal, two other girls wiped the lurid paint from their nipples and joined their wailing to hers. Like falling sparrows, the girls dropped, one by one and in suddenly devout pairs, to their knees at Marsman's feet.

Gently, he touched their heads as if he were anointing them. Thus engaged, he failed to note Superstud's appearance from behind the bleachers where the camp-following women were seated while absorbing the lesson being taught in this, their leader's latest foray among enemies.

"What the hell is going on here?" Superstud exclaimed in surprise at the sight of his wailing women.

"Salvation!" Marsman replied. "A necessary and complete surrender!"

"Get on your backs where you belong!" Superstud cried, seizing the girls by their shoulders and long locks as he sought to shake some sense into their heads. "Toss your legs in the air!"

Marsman smiled triumphantly as the girls broke free with protests about their lost innocence and the truly difficult paths of glory. While Superstud raged in his impotent and frantic anger, Marsman dispensed ashes, which the girls promptly used to mar their beautiful faces and bodies. He handed out sackcloth which they gratefully donned.

"But I have brought you a circus," Superstud wailed to them. "Jugglers I have summoned, ladies. *Clowns!*"

Smith glanced in the direction Superstud was sadly pointing. "Rachel," he whispered. "Look!"

As he and Rachel stared, male acrobats tumbled energetically down the steep incline of the hill. Female simulacra with brilliant feathers balanced on their pert noses pranced across the grass toward them.

"Come on!" Smith said, grabbing Rachel's hand and moving stealthily toward the troupe of circus performers Superstud had engaged to entertain his harem.

"Smith, what—?"

"It's time to escape the madness of Marsman. Follow me and keep quiet."

He dragged Rachel after him, careful not to attract Marsman's attention as he made his way into the colorful midst of the bouncing, twirling, topsy-turvying, leaping, flying performers.

"Now is not the time," Marsman intoned solemnly, "for frivolity. Now is the time for meditation and moroseness."

"Great graven gods!" Superstud moaned, clasping his head in his hands and then releasing it to test a kiss on the dry lips of a depressingly unresponsive girl who had come to Marsman a houri and had been transformed by the simulacrum's successful attack into a bleak nun.

Superstud argued vehemently with his girls, telling them that they must throw off the chains of their oppressor, that they must arise and revolt against his seductions.

Marsman warned them in an equally stentorian voice to avoid the traps that desire set for such weak creatures as themselves.

Smith, darting among the members of the circus, tore a purple cape from the ringmaster's shoulders and wrapped Rachel in it. He stole the rhinestoned tiara worn by a lovely trapeze artist and placed it on her head. He convinced a clown to surrender his red fright wig which he promptly placed on his own head. Quickly doffing his armor, he traded it for the red polka-dotted suit the clown was wearing, which he quickly donned.

Into the center of the group of acrobats he ran, after placing Rachel astride a jauntily plumed pony. He leaped into the air and was caught as he had expected to be caught in the skilled hands of one of the acrobats. The acrobat tossed him to a colleague who bore Smith about on his shoulders.

"Away!" Marsman shouted to the performers who were erupting all over the greensward. "This is now a holy place where lust has been slain and where tears of guilt have watered its obscene grave. Away, I say!"

The simulacra began to move off up the side of the hill, shouting happily to one another, performing their muscular magics and displaying their gaudy talents.

"Smith!" Marsman shouted, turning toward the bleachers where the wet-eyed women sat in sick humility, their knees pressed chastely together, their hands folded piously in their calm laps.

When he received no answer, he lumbered over to the bleachers. "Where is he?" he snarled at the women.

Only their penitent sobs answered him.

"Smith!" he yelled, his hands cupped around his mouth to turn it into a loud trumpet.

"Go back to your battles, Marsman," Superstud pleaded. "Leave me to my pleasures, please."

"He was *here!*" Marsman muttered. "He was *mine!* So was the woman—Rachel!"

"I might as well enter a monastery," Superstud mourned, slumping to the ground and cradling his head in his hands. "Marsman, you've corrupted my previously playful companions. But monastic amusements are definitely not to my taste. Boys bore me. Altogether too decadent."

"Smith!" Marsman called again, ignoring Superstud. "I enslaved you, and a master without a slave is no master at all. A general without subordinate soldiers is no real commander! Smith, come back to me. I *need* you!"

"It will take weeks for them to get over this," Superstud complained to himself as he stared in disgust at the girls who had begun to murmur among themselves of lost virginity and other awful martyrdoms. "Meanwhile, I shall starve on a diet that eliminates ecstasy."

"I will wage war on you, Smith!" Marsman roared, shaking both of his fists in the air. "The day will come when I will find you again and when I do my wrath shall make you and your woman bleed!"

"Even mad dogs have their day," Superstud shot at him bitterly.

Silhouetted against the sun on the hilltop, the acrobats tossed their new-found clown in the air. His laughter drifted down into the valley as the lovely bareback rider in tiara and purple ringmaster's cloak rode gracefully away with him, not once looking back.

Chapter 5

DOWN THE HILL and along a smooth plain came the circus performers, Smith a sun in the sky above them all as the acrobats tossed and retossed him, dizzying him with freedom. His laughter rolled in the air about him, another wingless bird.

Rachel rode her pony in the midst of the throng, her eyes on Smith as he spun about far above her.

"Rachel!" he called out breathlessly. "When I was a child, I—."

She waited for him to continue but instead of completing his sentence, he asked the acrobats to place him on the ground, which they promptly did. He leaned on the shoulders of two of them in sequined tights and velvet neckbands as he sought to regain both his breath and equilibrium.

Rachel dismounted and came up to him. "Smith, you were about to say something—it was about your childhood. What was it?"

He shook his head. "I don't know. For a moment, I thought I remembered another circus. Yes, a different circus with clowns and—and bareback riders!" he concluded, reaching out and taking her hands to twirl around with her, a grin on his face to hide the despair he felt over the escape from his consciousness of the half-formed memory that had just vanished from the screen of his mind, leaving it once again nearly blank.

Rachel, he noticed, looked disappointed, as if it had been she herself who had almost grasped a piece of the past only to have it squirm fishlike through her clutching hands.

"Well, at least we have escaped Marsman," Smith observed, releasing her.

She looked about her at the circus simulacra who were quiet now as if waiting for someone to come and tell them what was next on their merry agenda. "But I wonder what it is exactly that we have escaped to."

"Why, to life!" Smith declared expansively. "Look about you. These simulacra are dedicated to joy and laughter. Marsman was obsessed with enemies, and such an obsession can only lead to death." He paused, noting Rachel's expression. "Is something wrong?"

She brightened and looked up at him. "It's just that—well, we still don't know who we are. Or even where we are."

"Ah, but we do, Rachel. We are circus people who wear polka-dotted suits and tiaras in our hair. I am a clown and you are an equestrienne."

"Smith, you know we aren't."

Anger surged in Smith but it quickly faded. He wanted Rachel to share the exultation filling him, only partly as a result of the dizzying trip he had just taken, propelled by the strong hands of the acrobats. Her seriousness troubled him; her reservations about their present situation made him uncomfortable. He wanted to be able to enjoy himself far from the company of Marsman and that simulacrum's dreams of death. But Rachel would not—or perhaps could not —participate in his shedding of the recent past. Perhaps, he thought, it is because we have such thin pasts. Perhaps she cherishes even her experience with Marsman. Maybe it makes her feel more of a whole person—a person with a history, however limited.

He asked, "Do you want to go back?" and was not at all surprised when she shook her head. He had known she would. "We can stay with the circus," he said, prompting her acceptance of their present situation.

"Yes, we could."

"Will you? Stay with me?"

"I thought you were talking about staying with the circus."

"I was. But I was also talking about us and our being together again. It's important because together we might be able to find our way back to where we began."

He saw a shadow darken Rachel's face momentarily.

"Smith, I'm not sure I want to find my way back there."

"But if we can return, we will *know!*"

"When we met in the Valley of the Maimed, I felt —I thought there was something wrong. I was going to run away."

"From me?"

"It might have been just the shock of seeing someone like myself—another human being. Yes, it might have been only that."

"Of course it was." Smith held out his hand and Rachel took it. He turned and led her up to the nearest simulacrum, who stood silently, his Indian clubs resting at his feet.

Addressing the juggler, Smith said, "We would like to come with you if you'll let us."

"Can you walk a tight wire?" inquired the juggler. "Have you ever been shot from the mouth of a cannon?"

"I could learn," Smith answered.

"Wire walking is not really learned. Such esoteric knowledge is born in the blood. Being shot from the mouth of a cannon is not like becoming an accountant or a plumber. It is a calling. A serious vocation."

"Will you help us?" Rachel asked gently.

"Our caravan is not far from here," the simulacra said, picking up the tools of his trade. "You are welcome to come with us. It may well be that you will find yourselves something amusing to do there. The pay is poor but the applause of the audience is a priceless treasure."

The juggler turned and shouted an order to the others gathered about and they all began to move away.

Smith, holding Rachel's hand, followed them, thinking of tight wires strung above the weird world in which he now found himself and of cannons that would explode in bursts of smoke, sending him hurtling skyward to learn whatever strange truths the stars might have to tell him.

As he walked along with Rachel silent by his side, he fought against the feeling that he was betraying both her and himself. He had no right, he argued with himself, to be moving so carelessly among the bright beings who surrounded him with the escape they called circus. Carelessly? No, he did not travel with them carelessly. But his cares were, for the moment at least, submerged beneath his desire to simply exult in the warm excitement that had captivated him. It was not that he did not want to know who he was and what needles strung with what strange threads had stitched the fabric of his still hidden past. But somehow and definitely he did not want to pursue that search for the moment. Could he not be allowed his present feeling of relief, resulting from his escape from slavery to Marsman and that simulacrum's calculated humiliations? A vision of Marsman's gleaming boots glowed in his mind. He saw himself kneeling before them, suffering from a disease personified by Marsman who towered so insolently above him. No, he would stay here with the circus, which he was convinced could cure his recent illness. He would accept the circus as a necessary prescription that would lead to his recovery and, once fully recovered, he could then set out again in search of himself.

But, he wondered, have I ever actually stopped in my search from the moment I awakened to the sight of that black bird hanging so helplessly above me? Had he not only minutes ago almost remembered another circus and another self—a self that was small and alive with delight as colors flashed and music sounded all around him?

Even now, walking to the caravan which he had just sighted in the hazy distance, he had the distinct feeling that he was moving toward more than a caravan, was part of something greater than just a circus. Was there a method in what was happening to him, what had happened to him? Was the circus that now engulfed him and with him, Rachel, one more bead in destiny's necklace? Or was everything merely accidental in this world and nothing at all ordained?

And yet, even in the colorful confusion that was the circus, he believed he saw order. Without it aerial artists would fall from their trapezes and equestrians would be crushed beneath the flying hooves of their uncontrollable horses. He decided that the circus world of which he was now a part contained sufficient design to keep chaos chained in some distant darkness, so that even that blind creature's grotesque howls would be muted and hardly ever heard, its hideous face only a dream of a dream.

He walked more quickly, so quickly that Rachel had to hurry to keep up with him. As they arrived among the painted wagons and the banners that were flapping in the mild breeze, Smith let go of Rachel's hand and turned in a wondering circle, staring up and down and around to see, to smell, to absorb with all his senses the essence of the circus. That bizarre and wonderful world was, he suddenly realized somewhere deep within himself, an image of a realer world, but one reflected in a crazed and distorted mirror.

"I," announced a towering simulacrum wearing a tall black hat and a blinding red coat flecked with gold buttons, "am Ringmaster. Who are you?"

"This is Rachel," Smith replied. "I am—Smith."

"Welcome to my world. Please return my cape."

Rachel slipped out of the purple cape and handed it to Ringmaster.

"Your auditions," he said, "will be held within the hour in the main tent. Prepare yourselves, Smith and Rachel, to perform. We tolerate no slackers here, nor do we have patience with the untalented. The coins that whisper their way into the hands of our ticket sellers demand that we present tip-top and top-notch entertainment. We listen carefully to their metal voices that tell us that their previous owners have exchanged them for gaieties and bright excitements. Remember—in the main tent. Within the hour. Be there!"

"Where is the main tent?" Smith called after the departing simulacrum.

"You can't miss it," came his reply. "Follow the odor of elephants to the cages containing no lions, then turn right and proceed quickly past the place where corn is popping, then double back—but be careful when you pass the dais of Helen of Troy— shield your eyes lest her beauty stun you. You can't miss the main tent, but then I've already told you that and I have no more time to spend in discussions."

"I suppose we'd better think about our auditions," Smith suggested when Ringmaster had disappeared. "If we aren't successful, it seems we'll not be permitted to stay here."

"I'm not sure I want to stay here," Rachel said.

"Why not?"

"This circus frightens me. Nothing seems entirely sane in a circus."

Smith looked away from Rachel's frown. He began to walk down the sawdust track that was bordered by booths above which hung signs that shouted at him:

THE COURSE OF THE FUTURE REVEALED

BY MADAME YESTERDAY

TATTOOING DONE WHILE YOU WAIT

Rachel caught up with him, and they walked past the booths, through the sawdust covering the ground, past cages containing pink and purple animals they did not recognize and through a labyrinth of wagons with chintz curtains on their windows and signs lettered on their doors:

GOD BLESS OUR HOME

ABANDON HOPE ALL YE WHO ENTER HERE

Following the overpowering stench of the unseen elephants, they found the place where corn was mindlessly popping behind a marble counter. Obeying Ringmaster's instructions, they then doubled back and found themselves passing a series of platforms on which stood, sat, or slumped a series of obviously damaged simulacra.

"Wait," Smith said, taking Rachel's arm. "I want to see."

She quickly turned away from the sight of the shattered body of the simulacrum sprawled on the platform nearest her. But Smith stared steadily at it in undisguised fascination. The sound of a coiled spring bursting through the bandages covering a nearby simulacrum interrupted his attention.

Slowly, he moved down the line of platforms past

the broken displays. There was a pair of simulacra lying in hideous union, melted together by some unimaginable fire. Next to them, a man stood on a single leg, supported by a crutch, bleeding oil from his severed limb.

"Crutch!" Smith cried in startled recognition.

"I sell small vials of my blood," Crutch crooned without bothering to look down at Smith. "It is useful, I am told, for healing the wounds made by love's little daggers. They say it will make flowers grow in sand. Satisfied customers claim it has no peer in adding a blush of modesty to a maiden's cheeks. Ten cents a vial. Three for a quarter."

"Crutch!" Smith cried a second time. "It's me. Smith!"

"How many vials, please?"

"I don't want to buy your blood. I want to—."

"Please go away so that serious customers may be accommodated."

"What happened to your leg?"

"It is a sad story which I will gladly tell you for a small fee. Do you have a dollar?"

"Dammit, Crutch, talk to me!"

Crutch bent down slightly without shifting his gaze, which was aimed at some distant point far above Smith's head. "My leg that limped—I cut it off after the slaughter in the Valley, and then I came here, since remunerative employment is difficult for cripples to obtain."

"You cut it off? *You* did?"

"Mere lameness does not impress people. But a missing limb makes even the most jaded customer sit up and take titillated notice. I am self-supporting now, in a manner of speaking."

Smith said, "Was there no other way?"

"There was nothing else to do," Crutch insisted. "Did you expect me to remain where I was among the truly and permanently maimed—among the dead? A man must exploit whatever assets he possesses. He must make them serve him on his way through the world in search of whatever oddness he calls success. The knife I used was sharp so the pain ended relatively quickly. Every day now, Borneo comes and refills my tubes so that I need not stop bleeding and risk unemployment. I have never missed a performance and, except for Helen of Troy, I am the star attraction in this freak show."

Smith stared up at Crutch. It was not his missing leg I noticed, he thought. Because I cannot see it. I notice the space left by its disappearance. I see the oil that flows from the hip to which it was once fastened.

Crutch, as if he had read Smith's thoughts by some secret method, said, "Philosophy deals in intangibles. I think constantly of my lost leg just as do all the apes that come to gawk at where it isn't anymore. I have become a philosopher as dedicated but considerably less eccentric than Professor Apocalypse."

"I'm sorry Crutch."

"No, Smith. If you must be sorry, be sorry for yourself. Your name and history are as lost as is my leg. But my deformity brings me profit. Yours brings you only pain. Now go away. Here comes Borneo."

Rachel cried out in alarm as a lean figure sprang up onto the platform from somewhere below.

As his head turned from side to side, Smith noticed the tiny dials set behind each of his ear lobes. His wet hair was neatly combed and precisely parted in the center. Spectacles with silver rims imprisoned his eyes and a sparse bush of a mustache sprouted from his upper lip.

"Will you buy a bit of Crutch's blood?" Borneo asked Smith in deprecating terms, dipping his ringless fingers into the steadily flowing stream beneath Crutch's hip. "It is a curative for snakebite and frostbite and it works wonders as a cauterizing agent for wounds suffered in passionate Saturday night brawls. Try it. It comes with my very own personal guarantee. Your money back if not completely satisfied."

Smith studied Borneo's glinting eyes behind their equally glinting spectacles. He examined the man's neat black suit. He marveled at the stiff whiteness of Borneo's shirt and the precision of his black bow tie.

"Sir?" Borneo wheedled.

Smith shook his head. "I don't want any."

"Smith," Rachel whispered to him. "Let's go."

Smith let Rachel lead him away from the platform.

"Wait!" Borneo called out to them. "You haven't seen my most presentable presentation. You mustn't leave here until you have gazed upon my miraculously beautiful and gloriously desirable Helen of Troy." He leaped down from the platform.

"This way," he whined in Smith's ear as he took his arm and began to guide him away from Crutch. "This way to ecstasy."

"Rachel," Smith said, freeing himself from Borneo's rabid grip.

"I don't want to see her."

"Of course you do, missy!" Borneo insisted, his voice staining the air. "She may even arouse hidden desires within *your* lovely bosom."

Borneo urged them on and Smith followed him, once he was certain that Rachel, although with evident reluctance, was following them both.

Borneo marched stiffly along, his back straight, the stiffness of his body and arms in direct contradiction to the fluid volubility of his speech. Smith kept abreast of him as they made their way past platform after platform on which mechanical deformities lay. Rachel moved slowly after them both, her eyes cast down to avoid the sight of the wreckage on the wooden platforms.

"Ten cents, three for a quarter," echoed Crutch's voice behind them as he continued dully to retail the only vital item he had for sale.

"Helen!" Borneo exclaimed. "A name elvish and —."

"Ordinary," Smith interrupted, becoming annoyed by Borneo's smooth enthusiasm.

"Elvish," Borneo repeated, undismayed. "Even impish, one might say. And *Troy!* Ah, there is a name to conjure delirious visions, dreams of marble cities struck saffron by the sun, housing delights not known since insane emperors reigned and jungles everywhere retained their dangerous secrets."

"Well, where is she?" Smith inquired impatiently, becoming bored with Borneo's chatter.

"In every man's heart."

Incredulously, "Where?"

"Why, right there!" Borneo sang out, pointing a slender finger at the throng some twenty yards away. "Look!"

Smith stared at the male simulacra gathered around the empty platform and at the woman who was mounting its steps. A moment later, the woman stood erect upon her platform, high above the heads of all those examining her.

The hair that cascaded down her back was more

than blond. It bordered on whiteness as if the sun had seared gold and turned it to something less and yet more, bleaching it into a haunting memory of blondness.

Smith found himself moving more briskly, eager for a closer inspection of the woman who stood so radiantly upon her crude dais. As he came closer to her, he saw that her languid eyes were only partially open. Were they blue? He couldn't tell. Her skin was as delicate as the sheer fabric of the gown she wore. Only partially covering her prominent breasts, it fell away from them in folds that shimmered as she breathed. A tiny black mark was evident on her right cheek and that miniature flaw on her otherwise perfect face seemed to accent rather than detract from its beauty.

Smith, without taking his eyes from Helen, seized the shoulders of the gaping simulacra surrounding her platform and moved them aside. He ignored their muttered protests as he fought past them until he was standing directly in front of the platform.

Helen's eyes opened wider when she saw him. She moved slightly, one hip lifting as she placed a leg to one side, her slit gown slipping aside to reveal a perfectly formed calf and slender thigh.

She stared down at Smith. As he gazed up at her, her lips parted and her tongue flicked out to moisten them.

"Helen of Troy," he sighed, almost oblivious of the fact that she, like her admirers, was a simulacrum.

"A clown has come to see me," she said.

Smith had never heard a voice like hers. It hinted of small bells ringing almost beyond the range of human ears. There existed in it the sweet sound of secrets whispered in opulent bedchambers after all the candles had guttered and gone out. He longed to hear her speak a second time.

"I'm not a clown," he said, becoming shamefully conscious of the garish suit he wore.

"Even clowns want me."

"I am not a clown!" Smith cried, tearing the fright wig from his head to release his long black hair, which fell down beyond his shoulders.

"I do not care to know what you are not," Helen said. "What are you?"

"I am a man who now knows what love is because I have seen you."

"Do you know the answers to questions?"

Smith nodded, feeling an almost desperate need to assent to whatever Helen might ask of him.

"What wears the mask of an angel in its infancy and the face of a demon thereafter?"

Smith pondered for several minutes and then answered, "Truth."

Helen's laughter rippled down to him. "A good answer, clown. But it is yours, not mine."

"What is yours?"

"Love wears the mask of an angel in its infancy and the face of a demon thereafter."

"I thought—."

"That was your mistake. Your heart, not your brain, should have known the answer."

"My heart knows only one thing," Smith declared. "It knows I need you." He gripped the wooden floor of Helen's platform.

Her delicately slippered foot moved forward and came to rest upon his hand.

He endured the pain as she pressed her foot down

upon his fingers. "I love you," he said.

"Remember my question," she advised him. "Think about angels and demons and what terrible risks you run in speaking of love to me—or to anyone."

Borneo clambered up the steps of the platform and stood to one side and slightly in front of Helen.

"Ravishing," he said as he touched her cheek. "Arousing. Do I hear any dissent?"

None of the members of the crowd spoke. And no one paid any attention to the appearance of Ringmaster, who slipped up to Rachel, clasped a hand over her mouth, and dragged her struggling away.

Borneo's hand rose and twisted the dial behind Helen's right ear. "Bend, my dear."

Helen bent backward, her pelvis thrust forward, her breasts pointing at the sky.

A sigh from Smith.

"Bow," Borneo commanded her, twisting the dial again.

Helen straightened and, holding her skirt just above her ankles, bowed so that her breasts fell forward, the material of her gown no longer hiding their nipples.

A moan arose from many throats, Smith's among them.

"Sing, dance, clap your hands, twist your hips and part your lips, *recite!*"

As Borneo's flashing fingers twisted and spun the dials that controlled Helen, she obeyed the instructions he gave her.

"A truly delightful toy!" Borneo exclaimed with delight when she had completed her repertoire. "A woman both seductive and submissive. Now it is time for me to undertake the collection of tribute from each customer."

One of Borneo's words rang in Smith's ear despite his preoccupation with Helen. *Undertake.* He glanced again at Borneo, noting his black suit, black tie, white shirt, and black and white patent leather pumps, which made him think of Helen and how Borneo had undertaken to—.

Borneo was truly, he thought, an undertaker—one who undertook to display toys for entertainment and a price. The man suddenly repelled Smith. His thin mouth was a sword slashing through the sickly morass of his face. His hands were worms defiling Helen's body. His words smelled of smoke from cold fires.

"—and prices must always be paid," Borneo was saying, almost chanting. "So step right up, gentlemen!"

An elderly man shoved Smith aside and sidled up to the platform to declare, "Helen, you dim the sun."

"Bravo!" cried Borneo, motioning the man away. "Next!"

Another man, younger, but bald. "In a Helenless world, life would be death!"

Helen's eyes, Smith noticed, were slowly closing. Her body had begun to undulate, slowly at first but, as man after man appeared and offered his tribute to her beauty and his desire, her writhing increased in tempo, her hands pressing against her body, sliding up and down, her head thrown back and little gusts of air issuing past her bared wet teeth.

When all the customers had come and gone, glancing back and yet forced to depart by Borneo's firm commands, Smith stepped forward.

"I love you, Helen," he said.

"Why?" she sighed, shuddering in her ecstasy.

"Because you are."

"A splendid and not at all clownish answer!" Borneo crowed.

"How much?" Helen demanded.

"Come, come!" Borneo prattled at Smith. "Answer her, please. You have enjoyed my toy and now her price must be paid."

"How much?" Helen shrilled, cracked bells clanging in her voice as her body trembled and shook. "How *much* do you love me?"

"More than you love yourself!"

"A stunning answer!" Borneo screamed, twisting Helen's dials so that her contortions increased. "A stunning answer to my employee's question!"

Helen let out a gasp and then a cry. She collapsed on the wooden platform at Borneo's feet.

Smith looked up in astonishment at Borneo's calm face.

"It is," the simulacrum offered, "but the heat of her desire that has momentarily consumed her. Don't worry. The toys I employ endure. Watch!"

As Smith watched, Helen stirred, sat up and then slowly rose to her feet. Her eyes opened once and then promptly closed. Borneo took her hands in his and began to lead her from the platform.

"Borneo!" Smith shouted, moving around the platform to the steps behind it. "Where are you taking her?"

"My amusements are not indefatigable," Borneo responded somewhat testily. "And Helen here is one of the most sensitive of them. Her delicate mechanisms are always strained after a performance. Her art is terribly taxing. She must rest. Step aside, please."

"Let me stay with her."

"You will weary her. You will talk constantly to her of love."

"I won't," Smith lied. "I promise."

Borneo's sneer spread across his face. "Her beauty has maddened others too. Come back again tonight —if you are willing to pay Helen's price."

"Borneo—."

"What is it?"

"Just now—were you talking of real men like me or about simulacra such as yourself when you said Helen's beauty has maddened others?"

"Other men, of course. Men as human as you are and just as absurd."

"How do you know about these other men?"

Helen yawned and leaned against Borneo's shoulder. He patted her cheek and commented, "We all have memory tapes. Helen's tell me so."

"Then she remembers being loved."

"Helen remembers needing love, which is not the same thing. Now step aside or I shall have to exact additional tribute and you are a poor man. I can always tell. Poor men are full of questions and complaints. They like to talk of fate and luck's infidelity. Go away!"

As Borneo guided Helen into the small tent pitched behind her platform, Smith thought of one more question.

"Borneo, what do you remember?"

"Toys!" the simulacrum replied. "Hours spent in orgiastic copulation with my creative imaginings. I remember bombs darting out of bunkers with a truly startling *whoosshh*. Planes, I remember, all pregnant with steel foetuses. *Toys!*"

Borneo and Helen vanished into the tent, and the flap above its opening swung down. But a moment later, Borneo's head popped out from between the folds of striped canvas.

"It isn't right or even fair that you should covet my toy. Play with your own."

"Who gave you your games and Helen's memories of needed love?"

"You humans are all alike!" Borneo snapped, his voice angry but his eyes not only alert but also amused. "Next you will want to talk about God. But I cannot. I have no choice in my ignorance of my origins but to be an agnostic."

Swish went the tent flap.

Smith took several steps backward, feeling both puzzled and intrigued by what Borneo had said in response to his questions. But both his puzzlement and sense of intrigue dissipated quickly as the image of the glorious Helen in her gown and loveliness soared in front of his eyes, causing the tent to disappear and the sky to vanish. Did she not know he loved her? Could she not feel it? He considered tearing aside the tent flap that hid his beloved from him but he restrained himself. Instead, he thought about plans and plots and was suddenly certain that his vast and overwhelming desire to possess Helen would give him the means to vault the walls of her stronghold and permit him his longed-for union with her. Only that, he felt, could once and for all bring an end to his questioning and his hunger for answers. Helen was the world, his world, and he would conquer it.

As he walked away from the tent that hid his delight from him, he became aware of music sounding from some undisclosed source nearby. It came somber to his ears, rumbling along the sawdust track beneath his feet and weighing upon the banners advertising Madame Yesterday's talents so that they hung limp and lifeless beneath its onslaught.

He walked along and then, without conscious thought, turned into the large tent on his left. He was suddenly engulfed by the music, which invaded his ears and nostrils, making him briefly weak.

The tent was alive with lights, and in the single ring beneath them a woman stood. Smith halted and watched the woman until Helen's face, which he had imposed upon hers, dissolved and he recognized Rachel. Outside the ring stood Ringmaster, a whip in his hands.

"That is all you can do?" bellowed Ringmaster, his whip snickering through the sawdust at his feet. "All?"

Rachel raised her hands to her face and wiped the tears from her cheeks. But the moment she lowered her hands, her cheeks again glistened with her own salty rain.

"Humans!" spat Ringmaster. "They possess such depressing abilities. Weeping, to name but one. No customer will pay to watch you weep, woman. It is a useless spectacle which solves nothing and entertains only the most sadistic viewer. Can you not turn a somersault or two? Make bears dance? Are you only able to weep?"

Rachel stood without moving, the lights striking sparks that drowned in her water eyes.

"Can you perhaps discourse on tears and tell us why they should be shed?" Ringmaster prompted, circling the ring in agitation.

"Enough then!" he shouted when Rachel made no reply to his query. "This circus has no place for you. Take your tears elsewhere. You may find a country where they are the national pastime. But here they are of no value and certainly not at all amusing."

As Rachel stepped out of the ring, Ringmaster stood aside to let her pass, his face clearly contemptuous.

Smith, as she approached him, found himself comparing her with Helen. Helen was beautiful; Rachel was attractive, he decided. Helen and Rachel both interested him. The significant difference between them, for Smith, was the indisputable fact that Rachel aroused his interest while Helen inspired him. To what? To commitment?

But Rachel was human and Helen was—. He didn't want to think about that difference. Marsman had been real to him. So had Crutch and Superstud and Borneo and now—Helen. They spoke in human voices. They looked human. Was that not enough?

Rachel halted when she saw him standing near the entrance to the tent. He was about to speak to her, but a shame he could not explain surged through him, preventing him from doing so.

Ringmaster's voice rang out. "Next, Smith! Into the ring, man! I will witness your behavior."

Rachel's faintly accusing eyes and Ringmaster's commanding voice forced Smith to act. He ran from the tent, knowing where he was going, knowing precisely what he was going to do and no longer concerned with any attempt at an analysis of why he was going to do it.

He arrived at Helen's tent and circled it warily, listening, a predator seeking a known prey. When he heard no sound from within the tent, he loosed a rope from one of the pegs jutting from the ground and carefully raised a portion of the canvas.

Helen lay on a couch in the center of the tent beneath a glaring neon light. Smith looked about but saw no sign of Borneo. He stooped and entered the tent and then moved quickly to where Helen was lying, her eyes closed, her breasts rising and falling in an easy rhythm. As he lifted her in his arms, her eyelids remained motionless. He carried her from the tent, cold sweat sliding down his back. Once outside, he slipped away into the darkness that was falling beyond the lighted caravan, his burden light in his arms, Rachel already little more than a memory in his mind where the flame that was Helen of Troy burned so enticingly.

Chapter 6

As the stealthy Smith ran through the thickening night with Helen's limp body held tightly in his arms, Rachel ran with him. A transparent ghost, she sped along at his side, pronouncing indecipherable indictments which he could not help recording in the guilty chambers of his mind.

He tried to exorcise her by telling himself that he did not really know her. They had only just met, and if he had seen her that earlier, accidental time as she slept in the glass case in the strange hall where little lights spoke their luminous monologs—well, such meetings in sleep or wakefulness could not be construed as involving any kind of measurable commitment. He was Smith. She was Rachel. The islands of themselves had no common shore and had been spanned by only the most tenuous of bridges. But, with his theft of Borneo's lusty toy, lying now in his arms, he had set the torch to those bridges.

There was no reason, he told himself and the forlorn ghost flying through the night with him, to feel either regret or guilt. He would banish both feelings as he would also banish Rachel herself from the haunted history he was creating for himself.

But—how?

"I can't remember telling you," he gasped to her

ghost, "anything that would strengthen our bridges."

"But you helped to build them. You took the only tool you had—you talked to me of our being together."

"I was only being kind."

"Were you?"

"You have no right to cry over charred bridge timbers and only partially forged steel."

"I trusted and was wronged."

"Show me the evidence," he demanded. "Name my crime."

Her ghost was about to speak . . . .

"Is it time?" Helen asked, opening her eyes to another darkness that immediately flooded them.

"I love you," Smith said.

Rachel's ghost vanished.

"It is almost time," Helen said languidly, wrapping her arms around his neck, unmindful of the sweat they found flowing there. "Yes, it is almost time. My need is a reliable clock. I trust what it tells me."

The thought came crashing into Smith's consciousness.

Time: 110100.

Once again he saw the flashing lights and their electric message he could not now, he found, clearly recall. It occurred to him that for a man such as himself, for one who possessed such a short conscious history, forgetting should be forbidden. He had so little to remember that what there was, all of it, every detail, should be graven upon his mind to ward off the overpowering sense of nothingness he had come to dread.

Time: 110100.

"Helen," he began.

"Take me back to my platform."

"You needn't ever again suffer under the eyes of strangers," he told her tenderly. "You're alone with me now."

She peered up at him in the darkness as his pace slowed. When he placed her gently upon the ground, she said, "I know no clowns."

"Sit here beside me," he said, dropping down to the ground. "Sit close to me for I am cold."

"It is not cold. The air is gentle."

"Warm me," he pleaded. "You can."

"Where are the tents? I hear no calliope. Why are these trees here? Was it you who replaced the sawdust with grass?"

He reached out and seized her wrists. Gently, he drew her down, held her close to him, trying not to notice the faint whirring, the regular metallic clicking that reached his ears through her flesh that was not flesh.

"Do you make people laugh?" she asked him.

At first, he didn't understand her question. And then, "I suppose clowns must." He paused thoughtfully. "There was once upon a puzzling time, a man who woke up in a mysterious box made of glass. He climbed out of it and then went out of the building in which it lay and he met someone who had an entire list of names at his disposal. That generous someone let him pick a name. He chose Smith. But that, unless accidents and coincidences are far more common than are supposed, was not really his name. But everyone called him Smith and pretended to know him."

Helen gazed at him through half-closed eyes.

"You don't find my story funny?"

"No."

"Then that proves I am not a clown, doesn't it? If I really were one, I would be able to make you laugh so that you wouldn't look so sad. Helen, call me Smith and I will call you goddess."

"Name-calling is a waste of time. No one ever knows anything about anybody—except their names—not really. The men who come to see me—they don't know who I am. They know only that I am Helen and beautiful. Take me back to them."

"I have taken you to myself, Helen. From the moment I first saw you there at the circus, I knew you must belong to me. I had been alone for so long, and yet, when I saw you, then only did I know what real loneliness was."

"There was a woman with you when you came to me."

"Rachel, yes."

"Ringmaster took her away."

"I didn't notice."

"Of course you didn't. I was there."

"Now you are here and I am here—."

"Smith!"

Her crying of his name startled Smith. There was a sound in it, a ragged sound, that unnerved him. He felt her fingers grip his forearms and he tried to smile at her, doubting that the darkness would allow her to see and be reassured by his benign expression. "I'm here."

"I must find the circus, Smith! Help me find it before it is too late!"

He felt vaguely annoyed at her. Perhaps he was not the most handsome man in her world but surely she could not want so desperately to flee him. And to what? To starkly painted caravans and the pungent stink of elephants? He must make her comfortable with him, he realized. He would touch her tenderly and speak pretty words to her.

"Helen," he said, "the grass is soft. Lie down upon it with me. The trees hide us from rain and prying eyes. Accept their shelter."

"Where is Borneo?"

"He's not here. You needn't fear him anymore."

"Fear him? Borneo? I never feared him. We worked very well together. We understood each other."

"He's not here," Smith repeated, an edge of anger sharpening his tone. "I am." He pressed her backward until she was lying on the thick mantle of shadowed grass. She made no protest but her eyes opened wide for the first time since Smith had stolen her from the tent where she slept. He struggled with his clown suit's corded clasps and at last succeeded in slipping his disguise over his ankles. Instantly, he was lying beside Helen, one arm thrown over her softly gowned body, the other inching under her back to lift her toward him.

"I knew," Helen said, "the minute I saw you. You are like all the others in your rough wanting."

Smith fought to control his impulses in an attempt to approach her with at least a minimal measure of gentility. But the blood pounding in his temples made its demands, the fantasies flooding his brain issued their orders, and obedience to both was the only option available to him.

Helen squirmed beneath him and then threw the thin gown that had covered her away into the night. She laughed, the confident laughter of a hunter raising a gun, his sought-after prey already captured in the thin crosshairs.

Smith, his hands on the inside of Helen's thighs,

shuddered involuntarily at the sound of her laughter. Then, before he could part her legs, she spread them wide. Her hands fastened on his shoulders.

He was unaware of the blood her nails had freed from the flesh of his back. He was aware only and completely of the curve of her belly, sloping down in its delicate rounding to the thicketed juncture of her thighs.

As his erection rammed clumsily against her hip, Helen let her laughter loose in the night a second time.

"You sight the target," she cried to Smith, "but your arrow flies blindly past it. Skill is absent from your archery!"

"Lie quiet," Smith told her, his remark more of a plea than a command as he desperately struggled to . . .

He groaned in relief as he found his way within her unguarded fortress.

Helen lifted her legs and twisted her buttocks so that he felt himself plunging deeper into her welcoming depths. Within seconds, he was rising and falling easily upon her. Her body released rich lubricants that made his assault an easy victory although he had not yet attained his earnestly sought-after spoils.

Helen clawed his back until more frenzied red lines streaked it. He barely felt their richness of pain as he thrust himself into her again and again.

"You love me!" she screamed. "You love to fuck me!" she screeched, her buttocks raging pistons between Smith and the ground beneath them. Obscenities flew from her mouth like prisoners suddenly released and, giddied with an unfamiliar freedom, run amuck.

Smith heard her words and was aroused by them

as much as by Helen herself. As she grunted and heaved beneath him, he listened to her rowdy litany and was amazed that a woman so dazzling could succumb—no, could glory—in such a complete surrender to impulses he had once, but only briefly, doubted she could even harbor.

Their encounter continued to make loud the darkness. A string of seconds became a rope of minutes that were suddenly shattered by Smith's silent explosion within Helen. For a time, neither of them moved, locked as they were in the starred vault of the night. And then Helen stirred, her hands pressing against Smith's quivering shoulders. She forced him from her and rolled away from him to lie huddled and sighing some distance from where he crouched, his eyes on her, his heart a dull hammer against his ribs.

She fell asleep almost instantly.

Smith crept up to her on his hands and knees, wanting to speak to her but able only to collapse close to her and wait for sleep to come to him too, so that he might share it with the one who lay so silent and needed beside him.

Two days passed during which Smith and Helen traveled without direction over a land of luxuriant vegetation and animals that peeped past leaves in wide-eyed wonder as the two made their way to no known destination.

During that time, Smith became increasingly disconcerted by Helen's raging wanting. She would stop in mid-stride and turn to him, her arms rising to capture him, and a moment later they would be together on the hard ground. When it was over, he would help her rise and they would walk on.

A third day had been born and was slowly dying. As they walked, Smith tried to talk to Helen. He spoke of her beauty and of the joy she had brought him. He pointed out birds flashing blue against white clouds. She seldom answered him and when she did, it was to complain of weariness or to express worry about where the circus might have gone without her.

The third time she expressed such concern, Smith said, "You don't really miss it, do you? The circus?"

She stared at him without comprehension.

"I didn't think a circus could mean that much to anyone."

"It was my life," she said simply.

"No single thing is anyone's whole life," he responded.

"I miss the men who came to see me."

"They needed you to put an end to their loneliness and to keep their dreams alive."

"I needed them more. You must have known that. I tried to tell you but you wouldn't listen."

On the fourth day, Helen fainted. She was walking slowly beside Smith through a forest of tall trees that hid from them the feathered source of birdsong when she fell. Smith was on his knees at once, calling her name, kissing her cheeks, thoroughly alarmed.

She regained consciousness and spoke a single word. It might have been "living." Smith was almost sure it had been "leaving." When she relapsed into unconsciousness again, he wept.

When his weeping finally ended, he examined her body not with the hands of concupiscence but with the fingers of an untrained technician in an attempt to find out what might have gone wrong with the mechanism that she was. But only ignorance guided his fingertips and his brain was dry of knowledge concerning what made the simulacra move in their imitation of human life.

No more tears, he found, were left to him. So he sat beside her unmoving body and wondered what to do about a sick machine. No answer came to him. He picked up a stone and turned it over and over in his fingers without really seeing it. He found another stone and placed his free hand upon it. And then he brought the first stone down upon his hand that rested on the second. Blood spurted. Bones twisted in protesting flesh.

He sat there without moving for some time and then he went to a pool that lay in the lap of a natural stone basin and bathed his minor wounds, knowing his sacrifice had bought him nothing, knowing the awful fact that his brutal magic had bribed no dark god.

"Helen," he whispered after some time had passed during which he decided that his answer to the question she had asked when they first met had been correct. Perhaps hers had been as correct; he suspected it was. But he was absolutely convinced now that truth wore the mask of an angel in its infancy and the face of a demon thereafter. "Helen," he said again, saddened by the knowledge of her truth. "You'll die if you cannot get back to the circus and the men who admire you daily. One man—one love—is not nearly enough for you."

Her eyes opened for the first time in more than a day.

"Your food," Smith continued, "is the adulation of others. Without it, you will starve to death."

She looked up at him, her expression both regretful and yearning. "Yes," she sighed, "you're right. Take me back."

He wanted to strike her. He wanted to raise a balled fist and bring it down to break her mouth and blind her eyes because he knew that her defeat was his as well. He was scorched by the knowledge that he, a man, could not provide the proper sustenance for this machine that was made in the image of a marvelous and truly magnificent woman. He was but one; the mob that had stood in front of her platform at performance after performance were many. A thought crossed his mind. A single crumb will not sustain one sparrow for very long.

He was merely a man and for Helen that was not enough. Whoever had made her, for whatever mysterious purpose, had ordained that she must feed on the hunger in the eyes of men—multitudes of men. Yes, he admitted to himself, I am defeated. So is Helen. I took her away because I loved her. In taking her, I risked destroying her because I didn't understand. Where, he wanted to scream to the quiet sky that in his mind was clouded with vultures, where does love lead? Thinking thus, he became aware that Helen's own answer to her question was possibly—quite probably—as correct as his had been. Yes, love could truly be said to wear the mask of an angel in its infancy and the face of a demon thereafter.

With sorrow and an oppressive sense of guilt, he picked up Helen and began to carry her away in search of the circus she required.

He found the chaotic conglomerate of caravans and banners, inhuman performers and audience by accident. After wandering with the comatose Helen a gentle burden in his arms for several days, he unexpectedly detected strains of music that came from no birds' throats. Hurrying, he reached the top of a hill that separated him from the familiar sound and as quickly hurried down it toward what he was now convinced was Helen's only hope for survival, if not necessarily for salvation.

He sprinted through the nearly empty lot, past the banners and the deserted stands and came at last to the platforms on which the freakish simulacra, Crutch and Helen among them, had exhibited themselves. Crutch was not on his platform. The other platforms were also empty. Helen's was draped in black silk. Someone had placed violets upon it, which, in their withering, had become more bunting black than purple.

He deposited Helen on her platform and, as he began to rub his aching arms, he noticed the sign clipped to the canvas of her tent. Stepping around the side of the platform, he read the remarkable words printed on it by someone's steady hand:

OFFERED!
A Reward of Your Choice for Information
Leading to the Demise of the Thief
Who Violated the Code of Borneo
By Stealing Beauty for No Better Reason
Than the Satisfaction of His, Her, Or Its,
As the Illegal Case May Be, Selfish Lust!

"Of course," commented Borneo, appearing out of nowhere to stand beside Smith, "lust is, by definition, always selfish. So your crime is an undistinguished one actually. But, mind you, nonetheless heinous. It is a crime of truly capital caliber. Do you confess?"

"Helen's sick," Smith said. "She may be dying."

"Do you confess?"

Smith hesitated, and then, "I confess to loving her."

"Now that," Borneo declared, wiggling a finger in front of Smith's face, "is a ridiculous remark and evades the central criminal issue. All the simulacra love Helen. But *you!* A *human!* Do you mean to seriously insist that you fell in love with a machine?"

Smith could only nod.

Borneo took a step closer to him and peered into his eyes. "The more I think about it, the more I pity you. Perverts are deserving of pity, don't you think? A man in love with a machine! My, my! I can't remember ever having heard of such a sick thing. You need a paramedical team to minister to you, not a jury.

"But wait! I remember a precedent! I remember me! I was once in love, and faithfully may I say in my unnecessary defense, with an adding machine. Punching its quaint buttons with their pretty little numerals was quite rewarding, I found, masturbatorily speaking. But perhaps that is not quite the same thing as in your case. Nevertheless. That adding machine of mine measured casualties quite competently and I was devoted to it and to the deadly secrets it told me. Perhaps I cannot cast the first stone after all. Perhaps you require a purer judge, one who has never known anything of the seductions of adding machines or the siren songs that hot line telephones sing to the twisted ears of certain listeners I could, if my memory did not fail me for the moment, name."

"Is there anything you can do for Helen?" Smith asked, gripping Borneo's collar.

Borneo slapped Smith's hands away in a tantrum of flying fingers. "It is probably too late. It is almost always too late for those who live on love. But let's have a look."

He climbed up on the platform after demanding that Smith give him a boost. He stood over Helen's contorted body, his chin in one hand, and stared down at her from his black and white height. He bent down and adjusted the dial behind her left ear. He cupped a hand behind his own left ear and listened.

"Can you hear that rattle?" he asked Smith.

"What is she trying to say?"

"Why, what anyone made in the image of humanity would say under such distressing circumstances. She is saying that she will never forgive you, Smith."

Borneo turned his attention to the dial behind Helen's right ear. "That *slink, slurf, slink* you hear is her indictment. It demands your death. Not even a machine wants to make the final journey alone." He straightened and gazed down at Helen. "Ah, and she had such stupendous gears! I hate to think what they must look like now. I dislike even imagining rust." Turning to Smith, he intoned, "Rust and old age make cowards of simulacra and men. It is the inevitable way of things. A semi-annual lube job doesn't help. Neither does Social Security. Not altogether, at any rate."

"Call the simulacra," Smith cried in a stricken voice. "Beat drums and play fifes. Let her admirers gather and revive her."

"This is, undoubtedly, an emergency, as you indicate. Drastic measures are clearly called for."

Smith was shouting. He out-Borneoed Borneo as he cataloged Helen's charms at the top of his voice. He shouted to the circus world of her fragile beauty and called for the simulacra to come and worship at her swiftly falling altar.

A few simulacra wandered idly into the area. Smith promptly seized them and dragged them through the sawdust to stand in front of Helen's platform. "Look!" he commanded them. "See how her breasts rise so rosy above her incredibly delicate ribs. Marvel, all of you, at her primal geometry that can make a studious mathematician of even the most uneducated and doltish man."

"The good old days are gone forever," complained one of the simulacra, ignoring Smith's exhortations. "Helen's had it."

His companion said, "Borneo, give us Aphrodite. There's little life left in this old girl." He pointed disdainfully at Helen's crumpled body.

"Yes, she's just about done for," Borneo observed as Helen's body convulsed violently and then lay still. He bent down, one ear buried below her left breast. "—six, five, four, three, two, *one*! Helen is dead! Long live my other toys! I shall have to call a priest." He frowned. "But priests are in short supply since all this and we began. Maybe Marsman can tell me where to find one, since priests, I recall, traditionally cast their lot with the military and fawn on fighting men everywhere." .

"A souvenir!" whined a simulacrum, tearing at Helen's thin gown. "I must have a souvenir of my unconsummated contacts!"

Helen's gown ripped. The simulacrum bounded happily away clutching most of it in his trembling hands. Others climbed up on the platform and fought over its remaining fragments. A scissors appeared and a simulacrum used it to cut most of Helen's luxurious hair from her head.

"Devotion is always touching among the uncivilized," Borneo commented mildly, watching the melee.

Smith protested violently that the devout would destroy Helen if they were allowed to continue their worship.

"*You* destroyed her, Smith!" Borneo countered. "You did so when you took her from me and from the men who adored her and who, through their adoration, provided her with the only sustenance she could either endure or prosper from. So you are the guilty one. I judge you so. I condemn you to—what was your other woman's name?"

"Rachel."

"I condemn you to Rachel. A fitting punishment since it is like condemning a man who has seen the sun to blindness."

"Stop it!" Smith roared as Helen's body was repeatedly pierced by the wayward scissors so that springs sprang, freed from her body.

"Stop it!" Borneo shouted to the simulacra. "I have invented other entertainments, even brighter toys, for you to play with. *See!*"

He drew aside a drape hanging to one side of the platform. His gesture revealed a ballerina in a frothy yellow tutu, her arms ellipsing above her head, her toes touching the floor. He flicked a switch beneath one of her armpits and she bowed and then danced into the midst of the many bodies flailing about and above Helen.

"Watch her pirouette!" Borneo yelled.

A few heads lifted and then immediately lowered. The ballerina danced on unconcerned, her silver slippers flashing in the sunlight.

"And this one!" Borneo cried, tearing aside a second drape. "A gypsy with two huge eggs between his legs to prove he has much more than enough machismo."

116

The dark simulacrum, his head bound in a bright bandana, a gold ring looping from his left ear, leaped out onto the platform and crouched there, his evil eyes on the ballerina.

"Two truly wonderful toys to delight you with their technological talents!" Borneo cried, sounding on the edge of despair.

Smith, momentarily distracted by the unexpected appearance of the two simulacra, stared at them in some wonder. He was barely aware of Borneo's swift manipulations, first of the ballerina and then of the gypsy. But his eyes widened in shock as the ballerina raised one leg at right angles to her body and he saw the sharp silver saber protruding from her slipper. As she spun toward the gypsy, Smith watched the man's oval mouth open and a bullet fly forth from it. Glancing up at the man's eyes, he saw the crosshairs that occupied the places where his pupils should have been.

"The battle eternal!" Borneo crowed, clouting the nearest of the gathered simulacra to stun them into attention. "The battle of the sexes! A delight to the eye and a stimulus to every betting man! Will the ballerina slice to ribbons her companion of the moment or will the gypsy in his romantic anger bring her down to a final curtain with the bullets he spits so accurately?"

Bullets streaked through the air. Silver sabers sliced it. None of the simulacra paid more than momentary attention to the ghastly engagement.

Borneo, in disgust, switched off his toys and flung them from the platform. "What can I invent to equal Helen?" he moaned to no one in particular. "She was my triumph!"

Smith sprang forward and tried to tear the simulacra away from Helen, but they successfully and energetically beat him unconscious with her arms and legs as they tore them from her torso.

When their final adoration performed in the name of memory was at last ended, Smith regained consciousness and got shakily to his feet. As he did so, Helen's head rolled from his chest where it had fallen and been abandoned by the simulacra. He recoiled from it and was about to push it away from him when a flash of metal attracted his attention.

He bent down and gingerly lifted the head. Trying hard not to notice its empty eyesockets, he scraped away the torn false flesh to reveal the golden plate that was fastened with two tiny studs to its metal skull. He studied it and the words etched upon it:

Helen Macabe
Disposition decision
scheduled for Time: 110100

Reading and re-reading the words, he remembered inscriptions and epitaphs. These words had something of the qualities of both, he realized, this thin plate that shone so gaily from where it was crucified on Helen's skull. He spoke several words aloud: *Helen—Time: 110100. Helen*—that was obvious. Dismembered and un-lifed, she lay—what was left of her, what had not been stolen by the simulacra—on the crude platform. *Time: 110100*—what? The lights on the screen in the great hall where he had awakened, he recalled, had delivered that phrase to him! But it meant as much to him now as it had then—nothing. And Macabe?

Superstud's words came winging back to him.

"They all had names."

Helen Macabe.

Helen of Troy.

"Borneo!" he yelled as loudly as he could. "Where are you? I need—*explanations!*"

No one answered him, unless the wagons that were beginning to move off the lot were giving him their own cryptic answer as they wheeled themselves out of sight.

Crutch came hobbling past, the wooden stick on which he depended for support making arcs in the air as he passed Smith.

"Crutch, wait!"

The simulacrum did not stop.

"Crutch, Helen is dead. Borneo is gone and—."

"The circus is over," Crutch said, "at least for now and here. But it will open again elsewhere. There are always audiences for the vicarious risks and contrived pleasures we provide. Someone will always pay to witness our horrors. There is absolutely no need to let bygones be bygones. Follow us, Smith. If you hurry, I may be tempted to make you a very special offer. *Four*—not three, do you understand?—*four* vials of my blood for only a quarter. Bargains should be the cement that strengthens a friendship such as ours."

Smith moaned. He gripped his head in his hands to stop the flow of Crutch's words, which buzzed in his mind but made no sense, only noise. He shut his eyes as tightly as he could, so tightly that he felt the flesh thicken around them in hard folds. His moaning rose and reached a crescendo as words and phrases cavorted in his uncomprehending brain . . .

They all had names . . . Rachel . . . I am talking about the man you are becoming . . . reveal to you

119

how I was born hungering, lived a tapestry of griev-
ous lies, and will die with no nobility, like a decrepit
beast who knows that it helped to create and sustain
the uncaring jungle which will witness its hopeless
death . . . prisoners dream always of escape . . .
Time: 110100 . . . Helen . . . Troy . . . Macabe. . . .

The feeling that finally overpowered him was built
of a fog and a pressure in his blood. It brought eu-
phoria at first and then nothing more as he fainted.

Falling, he dropped Helen's head, which he had
been holding, and it and the rest of the world rolled
mercifully away from him for a time.

But the time ended with the arrival of an image of
a black bird flapping away from him as he called out
to it to please, just for a moment, stay and let him
decipher the message the giant clock clenched in its
great beak was trying to tell him. But the uncaring
bird swooped up and away from him. A thunderous
ticking was all that it left behind and it was soon
drowned by a tune that he did not recognize or wish
to hear.

"Tum, *ta,* ta," went the rhythm. "Ta, *ta,* tum-tum-
tum-*taaaa.*"

Resonant it was yet trilling. The bird's voice?

He opened his eyes and promptly shut them. The
bird was still there, in the world beyond the closed
doors of his eyelids. He waited. It would go away.
Birds, he supposed, had their business and were unable not to be about it. He only had to wait . . .

He opened his eyes again. The bird's face bobbed
in front of him. Its unusually large eyes glared into
his. Its talons touched its chin and its squalk shrieked
. . .

"Tum, *ta,* ta," sang the bird as it examined Smith.
"Ta, ta, *tum!*"

He rolled away and covered his aching head with his hands.

"It's no use pretending anymore. You're not dead. But she is, most definitely and, some might say, unfortunately. Wake up and I will pay you a fair price for what little is left of the sad lady."

Smith risked an over-the-shoulder glance at the talking bird and saw that it was not a bird at all but an old man—a simulacrum.

His hair frizzed grayly about his ears and temples. His equally gray skin sagged ponderously on his face. He wore garments of rags and what might have been scraps of banners—or flags. Stars glowed on them. Stripes marched across them. Crescents surged on them. Suns raged upon them. Wool, satin, silk, felt, velvet—the bird that was not a bird wore them all, and they all eyed Smith with glorious colors and fancy designs.

"Go away," Smith murmured, returning his head to the refuge of his arms.

"Oh, I shall, I shall. I always go away. If I did not, I would remain stuck in one place and no man with ambitions or plans can do that, now can he? Well, perhaps he could if he wished not to prosper or was intent on becoming a flagpole. Or a monument to himself or others. But not me. I go away all the time. Come, come, are you broken too? Is that why your eyes won't stay open and your arms are in love with your head?"

Smith chanced another glance and then he promptly sat up and wrapped his arms around his knees as he stared at his new companion. "You—you're broken?"

"No, I'm Professor Apocalypse. But don't let the name fool you for a minute. It means exactly what it

121

says. We are all doomed, every last one of us. It is only a matter of time and opportunity."

"I could have sworn you said you were broken."

"Did I say that?" The Professor tapped his forehead. "My circuits are unhitched or unhinged, I'm not quite sure which. Would you mind terribly?"

He beckoned to Smith as he unscrewed one of his ears.

"Take a look, do. My red wires are only supposed to be spliced with red wires. Are they? I think such strange thoughts sometimes that I'm almost convinced a blue wire has gotten involved where it shouldn't and made me think about damnations and five-day bicycle races."

Smith rose and peered into the deep cavity on the earless side of the Professor's head. "What do you want me to do with the blue wire that's tangled up in all the red ones?"

"Rip the interloper out! It has no business!"

Smith reached inside the Professor's head and took the blue wire between his thumb and index finger. The electric shock he experienced was mild, but nevertheless he quickly withdrew his hand.

"Here," said the Professor. He rummaged among his several layers of clothes and came up with a glove in the shape of a paw. "Use this as insulation."

Smith managed to slip the glove over his hand but he found that the four-digited covering impeded the movement of his thumb. Despite the difficulty, he at last managed to tear free the blue wire of which the Professor had complained.

"Ah, that's much better," the Professor sighed as he replaced his ear. "I thank you very much. Now I can't think of a single unimportant thing. When it finally gets to be Time: 110100, I shall be fully protected from any possible unpleasantnesses thanks to the kindness of a total stranger, a truly remarkable situation when you come to think of it, as I am doing at the moment."

"What are you going to do with that?" Smith asked despite himself as the Professor aimlessly tossed Helen's head in his aged hands.

"Well, I really don't know. But it just might come in handy someday. Humans, just between you and me, are always losing theirs."

"I'm human."

"You don't say? Well, of course you do. I just heard you. Do you want it?"

Smith tossed the horrifying object back to the Professor the minute it hit his hands. "No."

"Then, you won't mind if I confiscate it."

"It belongs to Borneo, I believe."

"Borneo has more toys than he can properly manage as it is. Are you a friend of his?"

"I don't think so."

"Of hers then?" The Professor held Helen's head up to Smith.

"Not any more. She's dead."

The Professor shook his head in chagrin. "Don't say that word. It strips the insulation from my circuits. Say she's broken if you feel something must be said. That's a word that is relatively easier to live with. What have you done with her arms?"

"Her admirers took them away with them—as souvenirs."

"Scavengers, every one. What are you doing here? Considering the fact that you're human, I mean."

Smith hesitated only a moment before replying, "I'm studying the follies of simulacra, which I shall then report on to my superiors."

"Well, why didn't you say so? So am I. A student, I mean. Would you like to study the ruins of Melancholymelody? You look a bit like an archeologist with all that hair and your hunched back."

"I want—."

"Well, come on along then! Melancholymelody isn't very far from here."

Professor Apocalypse put his fingers to his lips and whistled.

In response to his summons, a cart pulled by a gray goat appeared.

"Get in!" the Professor urged Smith.

"It has three wheels on one side and only two on the other," Smith observed.

"Would you prefer that it had three on each side? Two on each side? It could function quite satisfactorily with only one on each side, you know. My goodness, but you humans involve yourselves with such idiosyncratic concerns. Get in!"

Smith stood for a moment without moving. And then, in a friendly tone, he said, "You can keep Helen's head if you like but I wonder if you have any use for the little gold plate fastened to it."

"None at all." The Professor, using two of his four-inch-long fingernails, pried the plate loose and handed it to Smith. "Now will you get in?"

Clutching the plate in his fist—a clue to the puzzle he had made up his mind to somehow solve, and soon—Smith got into the cart.

The goat turned and gave him an annoyed glance before trotting off toward the horizon in response to the Professor's vigorous tugging on its reins.

Chapter 7

"I TRY TO OFFER my colleagues what homilies seem appropriate to their situations," said the Professor as the goat slowed to a creep and the cart stopped the violent bobbing that had threatened at times to overturn it. "I relate effects to causes as best I can despite my blue-wired infirmity. But Marsman, for example, pays attention not to me but to the loud voice of war. I have told him and told him that war is good for nothing but creating widows and making rich the manufacturers of prosthetic devices. But he pays me no attention."

"Perhaps it is because he hears the call of duty," Smith commented, feeling an inexplicable need to defend Marsman.

"Perhaps," the Professor agreed. "He is, after all, a man who honors honor. He is loyal to loyalty. Admirable qualities, I sometimes suppose, but I do wish he would seriously consider daisies."

Smith, gripping the rocking sides of the cart, turned a surprised glance on his companion.

Noting Smith's expression, the Professor said, "Daisies make one consider devastation in a larger perspective. One must be aware of sacrifices and their cost—slaughtered flowers, for example—before one can make decisions which, admittedly, may not be intelligent ones in terms of long range results but which can at least be bolstered by rationalizations resulting from anticipated eventualities."

"Who is Superstud?"

"Who can say," replied the Professor, not at all disconcerted by Smith's changing the subject. "I've had the displeasure of his acquaintance but I don't really mix socially with him. I'm far too old to participate in his amusements."

"I meant—." Smith halted, wondering exactly what it was he did mean. He opened his fist and stared down at the gold plate that was wet with his hand's sweat. *Helen Macabe.* "I meant that Helen—."

"Ah, yes," sighed the Professor, leaning over to pat her head as it rolled about on the bottom of the cart. "Helen. Women do have their place in our grand scheme of things."

"I meant," Smith continued, "that Borneo called her Helen of Troy. But this—," he held up the plate for the Professor to see, "—calls her Helen Macabe."

"An identity crisis obviously. Who are you going to believe? Borneo or that cheap fourteen carat doodad? We all chose our own names, you know. We think they fit our personalities."

"She has to be one or the other," Smith insisted.

"Or both. It all depends upon what you want and are able to believe."

"I want to know where she came from—who made her. Who made Superstud and Crutch—and you?"

"Obviously you are, like me, a philosopher, in your concern for origins. Watch out! Fallen tree a few feet ahead."

The Professor drew briskly on the reins but the goat, instead of swerving out of the way of the leafy obstruction lying across its path, lowered its head and butted the tree furiously. The cart in turn butted up against the goat's rump. The goat gave a bleat, and Smith gave a shout as he was thrown to one side and his head slammed against the side of the cart with a loud *crick*.

He didn't lose consciousness but for a time there was a redness in front of his eyes, a sea of redness in which Professor Apocalypse swam limbed instead of finned as he nervously expressed his regret concerning the accident and flayed the goat with recriminations to which it did not respond. Instead, it munched contentedly on the berries made available by the tree's fall.

"A man must always be prepared for the unexpected," the Professor advised, taking Smith's pulse and feeling his forehead. "Insurance is definitely recommended although usually expensive. Are you quite all right now, my fellow philosopher?" A reassuring chuckle was followed by an erratic electric sparking behind both of the Professor's eyeballs.

"I have no time for philosophy," Smith snapped. "I'm a man of action!"

"Do you feel better now? I know something about the repair and maintenance of red wires. Not much, but I get by. However, blood vessels and neurons are not at all in my line. Perhaps you should consult a doctor of medicine instead of me. I could give you a dose of Schopenhauer or a prescription of Sartre to be taken after every meal, but I don't think it would do what's wrong with you a single bit of good."

"Professor, you're confusing me!"

"Some of my very best friends are confused. After you've had a rest, you won't feel so uncertain. That was a nasty crack on the head you just received. But you're bearing up bravely. And now we really must be getting on if we are to arrive at the ruins of Melancholymelody before the sun sets. You will have ample time to rest when we reach our destination. And there at least I will not be subject to the ridicule of such as Superstud."

"He ridicules you?"

"Why shouldn't he, since he is a man of action and little thought and I am a man of much thought and little action. He loves what he can touch." A giggle. "I worship what I can imagine." A gasp. "He is young. I am old."

Helen Macabe, Smith thought. "What can you remember about Helen of Troy, Professor?"

"From what I've heard, she practiced industry and thrift. She was industrious in soliciting male attention and quite thrifty in hoarding it. Helen was a practical woman not altogether unphilosophical. That is to say, she believed in lies because she knew the truth and couldn't tolerate it."

"You met her?"

"No, but I do seem to remember her. I also remember how Nietzsche led to the Nazis and Leopold and Loeb. For which Nietzsche could not, of course, be blamed. Philosophy, my dear friend, is a tree. Anyone can pick and eat its fruit. The fruit cannot be blamed for being eaten. The eaters, on the other and opposite hand, can most definitely be blamed for their poor digestions."

"Helen Macabe," Smith began warily, unsure of what he wanted to say. "Helen Macabe was never with the circus."

"Helen Macabe. Helen of Troy. Have her your way."

The Professor got out of the cart, walked up to the goat, and kicked it soundly in the buttocks. Returning to the cart, he declared, "One circus is very much like another."

Smith groaned. "Now what the hell is that supposed to mean? Don't play games with me, Professor!"

"I won't. There isn't time. And it wasn't a game, what I said. It was a statement of indisputable fact, my friend, and you would do well to believe it."

"Professor, how old are you?"

"Clarify your question, please. Do you want to know how old I am or do you want to know how old I remember being?"

Smith was confused by the Professor's question. "Well, both. I want to know how old you are and, I guess, also how old you remember being."

"I am hundreds of years old. I've lost count of the centuries that have passed since I was born. But I remember being only seventy-one years old. The latter age is the more significant one because it is such recollections which keep me humming, those damned blue wires notwithstanding."

The Professor's mention of his infirmity almost escaped Smith. Certainly, its possibilities escaped him. But, as the Professor unscrewed his ear and placed an exploring finger into the wired cavity thus revealed, an idea occurred to him.

"Professor, aren't you feeling well?" he asked.

"Are you sure you removed that blue bastard? I hear a clicking inside me somewhere. It is a foreign sound without a doubt."

"Let me check for you."

Smith helped the Professor climb back into the cart, and then by kneeling on the wooden seat and bending forward, he was able to examine the wires inside the Professor's skull left exposed as a result of the simulacrum's unscrewing of his ear. He wasn't sure what it was he was looking for, but when he found it minutes later, he recognized it almost at once. Keeping up a running commentary on the untrustworthiness of blue wires in a red circuit system, he flicked the switch he had found—the one labeled *Feedback Control*—that lay just behind the photoelectric cell that served the Professor as an eyeball.

The Professor let out a sigh and collapsed against Smith who listened carefully to the series of sputterings that erupted from the one-eared head.

The sputterings gave way to the sound of relays clicking into position. The second sound, in time, gave way to a third—that of a muted, almost dreamlike version of the Professor's solemn voice.

"—the Institute offered scholarly men like me a chance to pursue both our own interests and our own inner selves. When this is all over, I'll go back to it. No. I won't. I'll go instead to—to Ibiza and let the sun soak the corruption from my mind and the sea wash my body clear of the taint I suffer because I sold my skill in philosophy and the exercise of logic to practical men. A major mistake. Practical men are dangerous. They cannot comprehend dreams, not even their own. They use their minds as merchants do—to achieve the goal of personal gain. Such merchants should be locked in their shops with their lamb chops and lawn mowers and not be allowed to put prices on the destinies of other men. Including mine—my destiny. Ah, yes, including mine. But I listened to their words and thought that the ends they sought might even be considered noble, their means to them at least not abhorrent when one considered alternatives. I always considered alternatives. It was my job. It was my doom. In the end there is, as practical men in the corridors and cafeteria tell me daily —no alternative. Given their practicality and predilections, I have to agree. Unfortunately, I have heard of hairshirts. They have heard only what clerics and prime ministers and the like tell them. Like me, they are destined to suffer the curses of the uninformed and the awful judgments of the dead. I do daily what I earlier agreed to do while the world whirls around the sun one more time. Ah, but Ibiza waits for me! Perhaps salvation does too—somewhere in another, gentler time."

"Who are you?" Smith inquired between unparted teeth. *"Who, dammit!"*

But he knew he would get no answer. A man did not "remember" his name; it was simply there in his mind as a piece of knowledge about which he rarely if ever thought unless asked. And Smith's asking now, he knew, could not evoke an answer. As he listened to the Professor's voice drone on about Ibiza and the splendors of the sun and the sea to be found there, he turned over and over in his mind the word "Institute." He had heard it before. He was sure he had. And yet, when he spoke it aloud, the consonants sitting strange on his tongue, no image of its referent occurred to him. Yet it was familiar. He must have heard someone say it at one time in his life, undoubtedly in that part of his life that was still hidden from him. *Institute.* Someone he had known had said it. Was that someone the one whose voice spoke to him now?

No. Because it was the voice of Professor Apocalypse that spoke to him, and the Professor was a machine as were all the other simulacra he had met. But machines didn't think. Men thought. Then what he was hearing were the thoughts of a man. What man?

Smith considered smashing the Professor's skull. He would, he suspected, find another metal plate beneath the covering of simulated flesh and on it would be a name. But he did nothing. If he destroyed the Professor, what would it benefit him? He would know one more name that he would recognize no more than he did the first he had accidentally found. It was an unsuitable exchange, he decided. He might yet learn more from the Professor, bits and pieces of some strange truth that would profit him far more than the mere possession of one more meaningless name.

A name as meaningless as Smith.

He gradually became aware of the silence around him, broken now only by the occasional mournful bleating of the goat trapped in its harness ahead of the cart. The Professor's monolog had ended. He reached into the cavity within the Professor's head and returned the switch to the position in which he had found it.

The instant he did so, the Professor stirred, his fingers flexed, his surprised eyes opened. "I was napping? Now? When there is so much farther to travel? I do apologize, my friend. Help me up. Let me put my ear in place and cajole my old goat, and we shall

132

be away. I do thank you most kindly for your patience. So few young people today will indulge an old man's weariness."

"Professor," Smith said, when they were jogging on their way again. "Where is the Institute?"

"The Institute? Oh, you mean Melancholymelody. I used to call it the Institute, but now I call it by a more suitable name. It's not on any map, you know."

"Do you miss the Institute, Professor?"

"Oh, no, not at all. One doesn't miss—one doesn't dare miss—what he has lost completely and forever."

"What happened, Professor, to make you lose it forever?"

"I fell asleep, didn't I?"

"I was referring to the time before you were made and I and the other humans, if the others are human, were put in those glass caskets."

"It's odd that you should ask. We talk about it often here. Crutch thinks that whoever made us won't let us remember. He says that persons unknown have eliminated that particular knowledge from our circuits. He may well be wrong. But, come along, my friend. Don't trouble yourself over unremembered incidents. The incidents a man can remember all too often cause him enough trouble to last a lifetime or two."

The Professor addressed himself to the reins in his hands and the goat at their other end. When Smith attempted to question him further, the Professor responded with grunts spat at the goat and occasional comments that had nothing at all to do with Smith's questions.

Convinced that there was no point in continuing to

interrogate his eccentric companion, Smith lapsed at last into a thoughtful silence. He maintained it until he caught his first glimpse of the shattered spires streaking up from the land below to pierce, it seemed, the very clouds in the sky. Silver they were. Gold, both yellow and white, adorned them and the combination, Smith thought as he stared at them, was not at all displeasing. The spires rose from cracked domes scattered across the landscape like eggs from which chicks, conscientiously pecking from within, were about to emerge. The domes were glazed; they glowed in pastel shades—pink, orchid, pale green, and other faint and unobtrusive colors.

As the cart came nearer to the spired domes, Smith caught his first glimpse of the stream that wound its curved way through them, flowing right through some and skirting others. Trash floated on the surface of the dark water—old shoes, crumpled cellophane bags, rotted wooden timbers, the stiffly lifeless body of a dog.

The moment the cart entered the area between the nearest of the domes, Smith saw the fallen heads which momentarily reminded him of Helen and made him look down at all that was left of her as it bounced almost gaily on the cart's warped floorboards. But the heads littering the pavements were stone. The bruised bodies to which they had once been joined tilted and leaned from grimy pedestals. He smiled briefly as he thought of how amusing it might be to join the head of one statue to the body of another.

"Melancholymelody," announced the Professor with a gesture in the direction of the silent city surrounding him.

134

"The Institute," Smith said sharply.

The Professor responded with, "Change is the only constant in life. I suppose a man must somehow learn to live with an unreliable status quo. I never did. It's no real wonder therefore that Superstud ridicules me. He despises the status quo. For him, it is Deirdre today, Sabrina tomorrow, and so on and on and on and on and—."

Smith reached over and shook the Professor.

"—and on," the simulacrum concluded complacently.

Distracted and annoyed by the fine ash that was falling from the sky, Smith began to brush it from his clown's suit. He used the frilled collar about his neck to wipe the gritty dust from his face.

The Professor noticed his efforts. "You'll get used to it," he said, referring to the dust. "The stuff is always falling. It reminds me of when I was in the Army and—."

"You served under Marsman?" Smith asked incredulously.

"No. Well, yes. In a manner of speaking, that is. That is to say, if I can manage to do so properly, I never served under Marsman but—. I was in the Army. You don't doubt me, do you? Doubts thrown in one's face tend to confuse issues."

"You *remember* being in the Army," Smith prompted.

"You're learning to get along here just fine, friend. Before long, you'll be elected President. You will be, that is, if you have enough money and the voting machines can ever be repaired. Not to mention the dingy basements of schools and churches where they appeared during all those Novembers."

"Who lives here, Professor?"

"Here? No one lives here. Here citizens merely exist. Melancholymelody—I call it the City of Cinders and Silent Troubadors. You've experienced the cinders, damn nuisance that they are, and perhaps you'll meet some of our songless residents in time." His last two words seemed to have pleased the Professor. He repeated them several more times. "Then there's Rachel. She's here somewhere."

"Rachel? Here?"

"Certainly. You didn't think I sought you out of my own free will, did you now? I prefer the company of certified intellectuals. Rachel sent me to look for you. I told her not to long for the unattainable but the girl is something of a wizard—a wizardess?—anyway, she answered quite smartly that she was sure that you were attainable and that such an attainment was most important to her. Now don't you tell her what I said she said. I've lost enough friends in my time without my unreliable gossip fracturing more of my relationships."

Rachel, Smith thought, wanting—almost needing to see her. But, as he thought about her, as he visualized for himself her body, the way her hands seemed never to be still—he felt that he could not face her. He had forgotten her earlier, able as he was to remember only Helen. But the Professor had just said Rachel sent him in search of me, he reminded himself.

"Is she all right, Professor?" he asked.

"She's alive."

"Is that the same thing?"

The Professor nodded to himself, muttered something, and reached out to pat Smith's hand. "She's

136

living in a house on Megaton Street. It's not far from here—just around the next corner."

"Professor—." Smith hesitated, looking around him.

"Yes?"

"Who built Melancholymelody?"

"Origins again! Can't you think about something simplistic for a change? Try religion."

"Whoever built this," Smith speculated aloud, "probably also built you. And all the other simulacra."

"There," said the Professor.

The goat lurched around the corner, dragging the cart and its passengers behind it.

"There she is," said the Professor, pointing.

Smith saw Rachel standing in the doorless aperture of the dome in the distance. His arm shot up, and he rose from his seat. He opened his mouth to call her name but, when she saw him, she turned and disappeared within the damaged dome that seemed about to topple down upon her.

"She's been expecting you," the Professor declared, getting out of the cart and tying the goat to a fallen statue's stone wrist. "Which reminds me. I've been expecting as well. Given the unpredictable nature of Man, what else can one do but expect and, if one happens to be messianically inclined, to predict? I'll give you a prophesy to take to Rachel, no strings or explanations attached. To wit, and I quote myself, 'As long as children care more for the prizes than for the cereal in the boxes on their breakfast tables, just so long will men and women continue to seek scapegoats and ignore love.' Have you got that, my good friend? I think I have. But then it may be a bit twisted, blue wires being as pesky as they are. In any case and/or event, the words are all there. It's simply a matter of putting them in the proper sequence. It well may be that I meant, 'As long as children care more for the cereal than the prizes in the boxes on their breakfast tables, just so long will men and women continue to seek love and ignore scapegoats.' You're welcome to the words, friend. When yours and Rachel's dry up and you sit together in an unendurable silence, use them. Who knows, they may help you to pass the time while you wait for my prediction to turn into truth instead of remaining just another postulate."

Smith ran toward the dome into which Rachel had disappeared.

"Where are your manners?" the Professor shouted after him, angrily shaking both fists in the air. "Did you never learn to give thanks for gifts given in good if possibly garbled grace?"

Smith halted briefly to fling a loud "thank you" in the Professor's direction.

"Don't mention it," the Professor yelled back, beaming. "Who knows who or what might be listening? Goodby! Remember me when your bedmates grow bored and wine tastes sour on your tongue. Apocalypse is the name. Philosophy's the game!"

Before resuming his search for Rachel, Smith watched the Professor sit down beside his cart, open a book entitled *Final Solutions and Other Anthropoid Ideological Advances* and begin to read aloud from it to his tethered goat, which uttered not a single bleat of protest.

Smith ran on and, reaching the dome he had been heading toward, quickly entered it. He found Rachel standing in the center of the large room the dome formed.

"Are you still Smith?" she asked him after a moment, her eyes meeting his.

"Why do you ask?"

"I thought that possibly—well, things happen to people and they change as a result. And because I hoped—." She left her statement unfinished and sat down in a chair in the center of the room.

Smith crossed to where she stood. "Helen is dead."

"You'll miss her."

"Have you found out—anything?"

She looked up at him and then out through the doorless aperture through which he had entered. "Yes. But you want to know if I've found out anything about who and where we are. No, I haven't."

Smith began to circle the dome's circumference, his arms swinging at his sides, wishing his clown's costume had pockets into which he could thrust his hands. "I found out what Helen's real name was."

"Her real name?"

Smith explained.

"Each of the simulacra may have a similar gold plate," Rachel mused when he had finished his explanation.

"Probably they do." He halted and turned to her. "Rachel, I don't know if I love you. I do know that I've missed you. It's difficult for me to be honest, because what I say now may contradict what I believed—before. But I'm glad I'm here. I'm glad you're here."

"Not even the birds sing in Melancholymelody," Rachel said quietly. "This city is without life. I came upon it by accident. I left the circus after you went away with Helen. There seemed to be no reason to remain. But I kept looking back."

"Professor Apocalypse said you sent him in search of me."

"He's mistaken as usual. I asked him if he knew where I could find someone who would help me to my feet if I should fall. Someone who would put a lighted candle in my hand before midnight came."

"He wasn't mistaken. Although he often is, he wasn't this time."

"If I were to ask you to hold me close to you for just a moment—."

Smith took her in his arms.

"I'm not a machine," she said, her breath warm against his neck. "I'm easily broken."

"So was Helen. The ones who loved her tore her to pieces."

Rachel drew back and studied his face. "She didn't just die?"

"She was murdered."

Rachel was silent for a moment, and then she withdrew from Smith's embrace and returned to sit in her chair.

A piece of the ceiling broke free and clattered on the floor.

Smith glanced up at the hole it had left through which the sun streamed. "It's dangerous here. This dome might collapse at any moment. Come outside with me."

"This entire city is dangerous," Rachel said. "It's slowly falling apart. Yesterday, the museum burned. The day before that, something fell from the sky and smashed the church steeple."

"Was anyone hurt?"

"No. There was no one in the museum. There never is. The steeple—well, there isn't a church, just the steeple itself. The entire city is incomplete. You may have noticed that there's no door on this dome."

Smith nodded.

"Whoever built Melancholymelody had no sense of the order of things. A steeple without a church, for example. There's a library here but it contains no books."

Smith pondered Rachel's comments and then said, "Could it be, do you think, that whoever built all this intended it to be incomplete? There seems to be, judging from what you've just said, a consistent pattern of unfinished elements."

Rachel stood up quickly. "I had thought of the same possibility. Melancholymelody's imperfection and slow deterioration seems almost planned. Even Fantasia herself, in a way, is incomplete."

"Who is Fantasia?"

"A simulacrum. She doesn't seem altogether real to me."

"Because she's incomplete?"

"Yes. She's strange. When I look at her or listen to her, she makes me think that whoever built her forgot to include some necessary part or perhaps left it lying dormant within her. Would you like to meet her?"

Smith caught the glance Rachel had directed at him with her question. It was the look of a temptress who knows that her very temptations might destroy her own goals. "Is she beautiful?" he asked.

"No, not beautiful. But she's kind and thoughtful, so she seems beautiful. She's in the garden."

Rachel walked to the door behind her. She opened it and stood beside it, waiting for Smith to join her.

He strode forward and she preceded him out into the garden that lay hidden behind the dome.

"What's she doing?" he asked, as he stood staring at the simulacrum with the short brown hair who sat on a small stool in front of a loom.

"She's weaving tapestries that she says are inspired by her dreams."

"Hello," Fantasia said, looking up from her loom. "Have you traveled far, sir? Would you like some cold water or some hot tea?"

Smith stepped to her side. "Fantasia, what is important to you?"

Her giggle was a quick fish darting past Smith's ears. "Importance," she said, "is as relative as speed, don't you agree?"

"Do you love anyone? The Professor? Marsman? Rachel?"

"Rachel is like a sister to me. The Professor has given me more predictions than I can ever possibly make come true. Marsman—ah, Marsman. In between battles, he remembers me."

"Do you love them? Answer me clearly!"

"I love life. Although lately it seems to be slipping away from me. My fingers are slow on my loom, and my heart only murmurs when once it sang."

"She hides herself," Rachel whispered to Smith. "She won't reveal her thoughts or feelings to anyone. She's like me in that respect."

"Like you?"

"I didn't try to prevent you from going to Helen."

Smith asked, "Do you need her?"

"Need her?"

"Is she important to you?"

Rachel made a vague gesture. "I share this dome with her. She was here when I came."

"If she were—gone—would it matter to you?" The questions he was asking seemed to spurt from his lips unaccompanied by thought. He wasn't sure what he was trying to determine. But he knew what he was planning to do, and so the questions were necessary.

Rachel said, "You're going to destroy her."

He nodded. Rachel's silence following his nod stated her assent, which he as silently accepted.

He picked up Fantasia's loom, raised it above his head, and brought it crashing down to smash her. As he did so, Rachel winced as if she were the one he had struck.

Smith rummaged among the debris that had been Fantasia. When he straightened, he put out a closed fist to Rachel.

She held out her hand, and he dropped the gold plate he had found into it.

"What does it say?" he asked her.

Rachel, in a distant voice, read aloud, "Rachel Kerner. Disposition decision scheduled for Time: 110100."

Chapter 8

"LET ME SEE IT," Smith said.

Rachel handed him the gold plate, and he studied the name and the ominous words engraved upon it.

"Smith," she said, "that must be my name."

"Are you sure? How do you know?"

Rachel raised both of her hands and placed her palms against her cheeks as if she were seeking to warm them. "I'm not really sure. I don't know. But I remember my first name—."

"And Kerner? Do you remember that?"

"No," she confessed and glanced down at the ruin near her feet, then she quickly walked back toward the dome.

As Smith followed her inside, he overheard her musings.

"I wonder who created the simulacra. And why. What is the significance of 'Disposition decision scheduled for Time: 110100?' When that time comes, what will happen to us?"

"There's no way we can know how much time has passed since you and I were put in those glass caskets," Smith said, adding his own musings to hers. "But Time: 110100, that makes no sense to me."

"Maybe it refers to time as measured in some way we never knew about or just can't remember knowing about."

"Or perhaps so much time has passed while we were sleeping that the method of recording time has changed."

Rachel said nothing for some time. And then she turned and asked, "Why do you suppose we haven't met any other human beings? The only ones we know about are those that were in the building when we awoke."

"If they were human."

"They were. I'm sure they were."

"There were lights on the wall of the building when I awoke," Smith said. "They formed words, some of which I read. But I was so confused at the time, so disoriented, I couldn't make sense of them."

"I remember noticing them too."

"I have the impression that those words should tell us at least part of the answers to our questions. We've got to go back to that building and wake the others. We'll read the words on the screen and all of us together will try to make sense out of them."

"I wonder if we can go back."

"What do you mean?"

"When will it be Time: 110100? It could come at any moment."

"And when it does, we will be disposed of." Smith stared at the plate he still held in his hand and felt a chill that made his skin contract. "Disposition," he said thoughtfully. "The word doesn't necessarily imply a negative result. It could be a positive one." He glanced at Rachel. "We'd better hurry. Do you know the way back to the building where we awoke?"

Rachel lowered her eyes.

"Neither do I," Smith said.

"I don't want to go back. Can't we stay here? It might be safer for us here."

He went to her and gently placed his hands on her shoulders. "Fantasia wouldn't have said she wanted to be alone with me either."

"That isn't what I said," Rachel protested.

"That's my point," Smith said quickly.

As Rachel moved closer to him, Smith's arms encircled her.

"We could take a risk," he whispered to her. "We could stay here together for awhile."

"When two human beings come this close," Rachel said, "there is always an element of risk involved."

"It's good to feel you so close to me."

"I wasn't talking about the closeness of our bodies."

"I know that."

Rachel sighed and tightened her grip on Smith. "You were right before. I did want to stay here with you. Now that you've come back, I don't want you to go away again. I know that's not a very flattering thing to say since you're the only man—the only other human being—I've met."

"Nevertheless, I'm flattered. I don't think we feel the way we do about each other simply because we know no one else. Even if that were the reason or one of the reasons for our feelings, it doesn't negate the value of what we feel for each other."

"Smith, I know now why I wept when you went away with Helen."

"You wept?"

"I didn't want to lose you."

"Rachel."

She looked up at him, a question in her eyes.

"Now that we've found each other, we're almost whole again. In one very important way, we are whole—we love each other. Even though we don't know each other's names."

"Names don't matter." She paused. "There may be other circuses, Smith."

He understood what she meant, as the memory of Helen flared in his mind momentarily. "If we should find another one, perhaps it will have a handsome animal trainer whose eyes will beckon to you."

"There are always risks for the person who lets himself love," Rachel responded with a slight smile. "Handsome animal trainers are only one of them."

"We should leave here now," Smith stated. "We have to find that building and wake the others. And we have to hurry," he concluded, his expression stern.

"Yes," she agreed, "we do have to hurry before a clock somewhere strikes Time: 110100 and—."

Her last words were engulfed by a sound that might have been a scream.

"Smith, what was that?"

"It wasn't a human voice," he replied, speaking more to himself than to Rachel.

"Was it a voice? It sounded almost like an explosion."

"Stay close to me. We'll go outside."

Together they made their cautious way out of the dome to stand on the fractured concrete surface of Megaton Street.

"Professor Apocalypse!" Rachel cried.

"Helen!" Smith exclaimed.

Helen's head was mounted on a stake which reared into the air above a black altar on which many candles burned. Her empty eye sockets seemed to weep as the torches that burned on either side of her severed head melted the remaining fragments of material that still partially clothed her metal skull. Within seconds, only the metal orb itself remained. As Smith and Rachel watched in amazement, smoke from the torches discolored it.

In front of the altar stood a simulacrum wearing a hooded robe, belted about his body with a length of rope and reaching to the ground. His genuflections were accompanied by the tinny ringing of a tiny bell held in the fat fingers of his right hand.

Professor Apocalypse lay on the altar uttering violent moans of protest despite the ragged gag stuffed haphazardly in his mouth.

The robed and hooded simulacrum took up a position in front of the Professor, who writhed helplessly in the ropes with which he was bound. Then, in one swift movement, he threw down his bell and picked up a knife that had been lying on the black altar's stained surface. The knife rose and then swooped down. It made its deadly flight a second and then a third time.

"Oh, *don't*!" Rachel screamed, covering her face with her hands.

The robed simulacrum turned swiftly, the knife held high in his hand.

Smith suppressed a shudder as he studied the fat face of the man staring back at him. Folds of flesh hung in garlands from his throat. His eyes were bright black slits. The hand that held the knife was a large child's hand with thick fingers and a palm that resembled a kneaded ball of wax.

"Don't?" he inquired, his voice a carillon. "The woman would prevent my worship?"

"He's only a simulacrum," Smith whispered to Rachel. "So was the Professor," he added in an attempt to calm her.

"I heard what you said," commented the robed figure. "You are quite correct, although your offered information is of little value to me. *He* is of little value as well," the simulacrum declared, pointing to the Professor's body, from which a filmy substance oozed.

"Who are you?" Smith called out.

"One who practices rites but one who is practical as well as mystical."

"Who are you?" Smith repeated. "What's your name?"

"Lord Ashmadai," came the answer as the figure turned back to his altar, the knife invisible in front of his body.

"I want to talk to him," Smith told Rachel. "Stay here."

She started to protest that she wanted to go with him, but at the mention of the knife she fell silent. As he walked away from her, Rachel wrapped her arms about her body, although the sun still streamed warmly down upon her.

When Smith reached the altar, he stepped to one side of it as Lord Ashmadai continued dismembering the body of Professor Apocalypse. Already a growing pile of gears and cams lay on the altar, all neatly piled and logically organized. As Smith watched, Ashmadai inserted a hand into the Professor's chest where he had slit it open and withdrew a strand of red wire. Setting down his knife, he began to wind the wire around one of his hands. A moment later, he ripped it free of its terminal within the Professor's chest and placed the coil he had created on the altar beside the Professor's other plundered parts.

"Why?" Smith asked.

Without removing his attention from the task at which he was engaged, Ashmadai answered, "My beliefs demand it. These rites embody my beliefs."

"What do you believe?"

Ashmadai gave Smith a covert glance and then turned back to his victim. "Even infidels such as you may be should pay respect to foreign customs, and yet you remain standing, your knees unbent."

Smith did not move. "I asked you a question."

"You also insult me by not bending your knees. If you have no respect for me and my rites, perhaps you have respect for the object of my worship."

"I knelt once to Marsman. I will kneel no more."

"Aha! You knelt to Marsman!" Ashmadai spun around and looked at Smith with new interest. "Then you are not a total disbeliever in—but I have not answered your question about my beliefs. Had you asked Marsman about them, he could have told you what they are. He and I are members of different branches of the same religion. He believes in sacrifice as I do, but with a difference."

"In sacrifice?"

"Was my answer to your question too clear to be believed, or do you find it too complex and therefore equally incomprehensible?"

"I understand that you have sacrificed Professor Apocalypse. But to whom?"

"To whom? Mystics sacrifice to gods. I sacrifice to concepts. Expediency, for example. Progress, for another example. These red wires will be stockpiled to satisfy my possible future needs. In the meantime, I will proceed to sacrifice Melancholymelody, stone statue by stone statue, dome by dome. This old fool is but a beginning. You may be another one, you who insist upon manifesting your infidelity by your rigid knees!"

"Machines are easy to destroy," Smith said quietly. "Human beings are a bit more difficult."

"You are not a machine? You are a human being?"

"I am. So is Rachel."

"Rachel? Ah, you mean that frightened female over there. Tell her to take her chances with unfamiliar ideas and events. Tell her to come forward and join our stimulating discussion."

Smith hesitated only briefly, and then he called out to Rachel.

"This is Lord Ashmadai," he told her as she reached his side.

"May I?" Ashmadai asked and reached for Rachel.

She let out a cry as she succeeded in evading his grasp.

"Let her alone!" Smith commanded.

"I merely wanted to examine an example of human construction," Ashmadai explained.

"What did you mean before," Smith prodded, "when you talked about sacrificing Melancholymelody?"

"What I said. No more, no less. It is mine, you know. Superstud was given his computer and his harem. Marsman, his skeletal army. Fantasia, her silent troubadors. The Professor was given his goat, and Crutch his beloved cripples. Borneo had Helen. Helen had her audience. Loman has his own universe. I have Melancholymelody."

Smith, at the mention of the name Loman, wanted

to ask to whom Ashmadai was referring, but he decided to wait for a more opportune time. His major concern at the moment was to comprehend Ashmadai's words and actions and by so doing understand the relationship of the simulacra to himself, to Rachel, and to the others still asleep in the great hall.

Ashmadai turned his attention once more to the Professor's corpse adorning his altar. The knife in his hand flashed in the sunlight. As Smith watched and Rachel averted her gaze, the piles of parts that had once permitted the Professor to walk and talk grew tall until they teetered glittering in the glow of light cast by the candles and torches.

"Now," announced Ashmadai with pleasure, "it is Melancholymelody's turn. No, not yet. First, Fantasia."

"Fantasia," Rachel said, obviously startled at the mention of the name. "She's—." She glanced at Smith.

"Fantasia," he told Ashmadai, "is—inoperative."

"Dead?" Ashmadai bleated. "Who killed her?" When neither Smith nor Rachel answered him, he smiled and said, "Perhaps you are not infidels after all. You too sacrifice as all devout acolytes must in order to gain their own ends. I wonder why you killed her. Well, no matter. We all have our motives for even our seemingly unmotivated actions, don't we? I shall salvage whatever of value is left of her. After I attend to Melancholymelody, that is."

"What are you going to do?" Rachel inquired uneasily.

"Do, my dear? Why nothing more. All I need to do, I have done. Now I wait with clean hands and a dedicated mind for the city to crumble as I originally planned when it was made for me."

152

Smith and Rachel followed Ashmadai as he strode toward the dome they had just left. They watched him take instruments from pockets hidden in his robe and make ready to use them.

"Calipers," Ashmadai explained, waving the steel tool in his hand and then using it to make esoteric measurements. He identified the plumb line and other instruments he carried while talking of calculated failures of even structural steel and prestressed concrete. As he talked and measured, the city continued to crumble. Sections fell heavily from domes. Statues tumbled to crack and shatter against buckling sidewalks.

Soon, Ashmadai was shouting to make himself heard over the roar of collapsing buildings. "All goes according to schedule and plan," he exulted as he pulled a rectangular watch from his robe and glanced at it.

"What time is it?" Smith yelled between hands cupped around his mouth.

"See for yourself." Ashmadai obligingly handed Smith his watch.

"Rachel! Look!"

An intake of breath signalled her shock as she stared at the strangely shaped watch.

"The lowest number," Smith observed, as he studied the list of miniature numerals that bordered all four sides of the watch, "is 108000. The highest is—," he scanned the face of the watch, "—110100!"

"But what time is it now?" Rachel asked, covering her ears to block out the riotous sound made by the fall of the spired and gilded library a block away. "How can we possibly tell what time it is when there are four hands?"

The four hands to which Rachel had referred

pointed at four different sets of digits, then shuddered and moved on in a seemingly random pattern that contained no discernible repetition of movement.

"Ashmadai!" Smith shouted, his voice encapsulating both his anger and anxiety. "Is it Time: 110100?"

"No!" came the loud answer.

"When will it be Time: 110100?"

"Soon enough. Too soon for some, I expect. But then that is the fate of those who would transgress against us and yearn to steal and eat our very own daily bread!"

Smith threw back his head and saw the sky, wanting to tear the sun from it, to pound his fists against something, to howl his frustration and let the sound of his howling blend with the grievous creaking and crashing dirge of the city around him. He had, for a brief but painful moment, a clear realization of what it meant to be human. It meant, he understood in that fleeting instant, to ask questions and to be answered with riddles. It meant to need to know and to have that need remain nestled within one's brain, always gnawing yet destined never to be satisfied, while chaos stalked about the limited field perceived by one's senses and order, blood brother of design, lamented unheard.

"Beautiful!" Ashmadai cried, performing a series of ritualistic gestures—touching his shoulders, his navel, and reaching eagerly inside his robe to clutch his genitals. "There goes the concert hall! Just listen to the sound it's singing!"

Smith heard the garish musical theme to which Ashmadai referred. It was composed of stricken notes made by twisting steel and disintegrating timbers, a tortured symphony.

"The chorus is simply splendid!" Ashmadai declared. "Hear how the silent troubadors sing aloud at

154

last and with such soul-shattering gusto too! Aha, here come the minions of Marsman to reap the spoils of victory!"

"Smith!" Rachel called out as a phalanx of skeletons rode into view at the distant end of Megaton Street.

"Run!" he yelled and seized her wrist.

"Wait!" ordered Ashmadai as they began to sprint up the street away from the skeletons that had dismounted and were prowling about the wreckage of the city in their search for treasures. "There is no need to fear Marsman. We are old friends, Marsman and I. I will intercede for you. Although he and I use different weapons—he uses brawn and bravado; I prefer brains—we work well together. I plan the battles; he performs their bloody ballets. *Wait!*"

But Smith and Rachel had already turned the corner. They kept on running, Ashmadai's words no longer even echoes in their ears.

"Where can we hide?" Rachel asked breathlessly.

"No one hides from me!" roared Marsman as he suddenly appeared amid a cluster of partially destroyed domes. His red horse reared up, its raised front hooves two hammers in the air. "We meet again, Smith! I am glad to have this new chance to eliminate you!"

Smith backed away as Marsman's horse quieted, his arm around Rachel. "I'm not easily destroyed, Marsman!"

"Had you not escaped from me so precipitously before, Smith, I would have succeeded in effectively destroying you, because the habit of kneeling sucks the soul from a man and subservience rots a man's heart. You have no weapon, I see. Then we will fight each other with our fists."

155

As Marsman leaped down from his horse, Smith stiffened, readying himself to fight and trying to banish the feeling of sadness that had swept over him as he stared at the pale face and haunted eyes of the simulacrum who was moving relentlessly toward him.

But before Marsman reached him, Lord Ashmadai came running around the corner, his arms waving and his chest heaving. When he saw the confrontation, he lurched to one side, altered his course and collided with a brittle *chinking* sound against Marsman who fell, stunned.

Instantly, Ashmadai beckoned to Smith. "Come! I will show you a place where you will be safe from my friend's boiling blood and his misguided omniscience concerning enemies."

"Where?"

"My home. It lies far below Melancholymelody. Marsman does not even know of its existence. Hurry, before he recovers and offers you death instead of a happier sanctuary. No, no! Leave the woman. When Marsman awakens, he will use her to forget his defeat. In his abusive usage, he may even forget you entirely!"

"Rachel comes with me or I remain here," Smith stated, meeting Ashmadai's eyes.

"Then let her come. Away, all of us!"

Smith and Rachel ran with Ashmadai, whose robe swirled about his ankles as he led them to a statue of Fantasia. Standing in front of it, he twisted the figure, which slowly swung aside on invisible hinges to reveal a stairway leading down into the ground.

"You go first," Smith ordered Ashmadai.

As the simulacrum eased himself into the opening and vanished down the steps, Rachel turned to Smith and asked, "Do you trust him?"

"No. But I'm not sure I can defeat Marsman. I suppose I shouldn't admit that. But it's true. For some strange reason, I would rather battle an entire army than him."

"Then you're saying we have no choice but to follow Lord Ashmadai."

"I'm saying that I would rather follow Ashmadai than fight Marsman. Rachel, I never knew I was a coward."

"I don't believe you are a coward."

He met her steady gaze for a moment, and then he helped her begin her descent of the stairs that led down to Ashmadai's domain.

As he followed her, not speaking, his mind still on Marsman, he became aware of the statue of Fantasia swinging back into place above his head.

Darkness.

Chapter 9

THE ALMOST TANGIBLE darkness into which Smith and Rachel descended seemed to invade both their minds and their bodies as they made their cautious way down the unseen steps beneath their feet.

Rachel suddenly cried out in disgust and seized Smith.

"What's the matter?" he asked, holding her tightly as her convulsive breathing rasped through the moist air.

"There was something on the wall. I *felt* it!"

"Lizards," came Lord Ashmadai's voice, welling up from somewhere far below them. "They and the spiders keep one another uncomfortable company here."

Rachel made a harsh sound of revulsion but, at Smith's urging, resumed her descent.

As they reached the bottom of the stairs, Ashmadai called out words of encouragement to them. He was faintly illumined by the gray glow that emanated from the walls of the tunnel arching above him.

"How much farther?" Smith called out some time later, as the long journey through the tunnel began to seem endless.

There was no reply other than the sound of Ashmadai's feet shuffling along some distance ahead.

At last, he announced, "Here we are!"

Smith blinked as a torch flared into red life in a room at the end of the tunnel. When his eyes became accustomed to the brightness, he stepped into the sprawling rotunda opening off the tunnel.

He noted the limestone walls and granite floor but what attracted his attention most was the huge mosaic covering most of the floor. In the center was the origin of what ultimately became, in its ribboning around and outward, a gigantic pinwheel. It was divided into units of equal size and varying colors.

Ashmadai, noticing Smith's interest in the mosaic commented, "It is a device of my own design. It affords me many hours of stimulation."

Smith bent down to examine the names painted on the squares into which the pinwheel was split: *Rotterdam, Peking, Londonderry, Melancholymelody, Philadelphia, Ottawa, Anchorage, Vladivostock.*

"Those squares, as you can see," Ashmadai said, his eyes on Smith, "represent towns and cities. The red squares represent countries."

Smith stepped forward and looked down at the red squares to which Ashmadai had referred. They were scattered at random points throughout the overall design—*Australia, Amerland, Eurounion,* and several others.

"That lovely green one—see it there—over there to your left? That one is the most important one of all."

Earth, Smith read. "Ashmadai," he said aloud.

"Yes?"

"Is this—are we on Earth?"

"As far as I can recall, yes, we definitely are. My memory tapes are in quite good condition so I would say that you can accept my recollection as reliable."

He turned away and began to move about the rotunda, walking just beyond the edge of the painted area on the floor, lighting torches as he talked.

"Only today it became Melancholymelody's turn. Yesterday—now let me think. Ah, yes. Yesterday we did not play. Yesterday was the sixteenth of August —my birthday. I treat that day as a holiday. No one —." His words faded.

"Did you say 'No one dies that day?' " Smith questioned.

"Speak to Marsman about death," Ashmadai retorted too loudly. "Speak to me of plans and contingencies. Marsman executes. I create."

"Smith," Rachel whispered. "He *did* say—."

"Silence!" Ashmadai ordered, waving his arms about in a frenzy of agitation. "You are in a temple, and reverence must be summoned to mind. On the walls you see the relics of my religion. On the floor—."

Smith glanced at the walls; maps, charts, graphs and statistical tables hung upon them.

"On the floor," Ashmadai continued, "is my proving ground, where my fancies and imaginations are transformed via practical alchemy and precocious wizardry into facts and other entrepreneurial manifestations."

"I don't understand you," Smith snapped angrily. "We talk the same language but your words make little sense to me."

"Yes, it is a tragedy," Ashmadai declared sadly. "I was born to be misunderstood. Some sickly star must have shed its pale light on my bloody entrance into the world. Even the blind union of the egg and sperm from which I sprang must have been cursed by astrological mismatings. That is why I now rely only

160

on numbers and probabilities, antiseptic words and possible events—not the vagaries of stars, planets, and other such astronautical diversions.

"I have never been without employment," Ashmadai continued with unmistakable pride. "Excuse me, but my hands are cold." He held them together near the torch above his head, rubbing them, blowing gustily upon them. "Governments invite me to official conclaves. Businessmen buy feasts for me. Even otherwise voiceless men call me on the telephone and enlist my services without flinching. I am indispensable to men who pursue such unattainable goals as security or a sound night's sleep beneath their skies filled with flying iron."

"What is—?" Smith began, pointing to the pinwheel.

"A game, only a game," interrupted Ashmadai. "One in which forfeits are sometimes paid and sacrifices always demanded of the players."

Smith felt revulsion well up within him and threaten to drown the self-control he struggled to maintain in the face of the bizarre events from which he had just escaped on the surface of that world which Ashmadai had identified as Earth. The simulacrum's eyes made Smith think of hunger unsatisfied. His hands made him think of ice; they seemed to send invisible rays of cold slicing through and chilling the air wherever they pointed. But it was Ashmadai's words that revolted him more than the simulacrum's physical appearance or definitive aura of evil. Those words rang throughout the rotunda, their sounds announcing information, but their meanings disguised and distorted.

"Would you like to see my game played?" Ashmadai inquired, his bowing body making its own abject plea, his voice a sly tempter. "It is not only amusing but instructive as well. I have always believed that pleasure by itself was pointless, if not actually sinful. Combine it with education, however, and one need seek no further for its justification."

"No," Rachel said.

"No?" Ashmadai's fingers coiled around one another, bloodless snakes in their airy nest. "I told you," he said to Smith petulantly, "that you should not bring her with you. Women prefer pleasure unalloyed. Instruction appeals to their brains, which they would rather let lie dormant like some hibernating nuisance."

"I'd like to see your game played, Ashmadai."

"Smith!"

"It's important, Rachel. I'm trying to understand —."

"Then you are a scholar too, Smith, if I may call you by your name. I trust you will not resent the familiarity on my part. But I do believe it is better to be friends rather than surly antagonists with those who share one's interests. Unfortunately, friendship is often not possible when the same interests are shared by two people."

"Can you explain what you mean, Ashmadai?"

"Oil fields." Ashmadai waved his arms upward. "Moon bases. Bananas. Copper. The list is long. But you asked me to explain what I said. Let's assume that you and I both love to wear copper bracelets. Yet, there are only so many copper mines. When you begin to worry about a possible end to copper resources and thus a beginning to the time when your wrists will go unbraceleted, antagonism between us is born."

"I think I understand."

"Sit, sit!" Ashmadai reached for Smith's arm, but Smith drew back and seated himself in the wooden chair standing against one wall. Ashmadai turned to Rachel, and she hurried to where Smith had seated himself and took the chair next to his.

"I used to long for the touch of human flesh," Ashmadai mused, standing almost forlornly alone in the center of the rotunda. "But I soon learned that if I could not manage to achieve one sort of touch, I could always achieve another. But enough of my ramblings. To the matter at hand!"

He fluttered across the colorful floor and threw open a door behind which stood many naked and unmoving simulacra. He seized one by the hair and tilted it toward him. As he dragged it to the starting point on the outermost edge of the giant pinwheel, its toes scraped noisily along the rough floor.

"I will activate this man," he announced, adjusting the dials behind the potential player's ear. "He will be our first gamesman. Now the object of the game, as you may have already guessed, is to reach—safely —the center block there." He hopped to the yellow square and tapped it with his foot.

"What does it say?" Smith called out.

"Why, *Life,* of course."

Smith and Rachel watched him scurry across the room, give one final touch to the simulacrum's mechanisms, and then draw back as the naked man lifted one foot from the first square and set it flatly down upon the second.

"Progress!" shouted Ashmadai, busily setting more torches ablaze. Their light revealed a scorecard covering a large expanse of wall and a complex of several miniature buildings hitherto hidden in the shadows dropping along the rotunda's periphery.

"The player still plays. He may even win. Why, look! He has already won a point." Ashmadai took chalk from a tray and made a/on the scorecard before turning back to watch his player's foot rise, hover, and then descend on the third square.

By the time the simulacrum had reached the fifth square, which was labeled *Prague,* Smith had begun to pay less attention to what was taking place before him. He examined instead the small buildings that had been revealed by the additional light Ashmadai had added to the area. They consisted of what appeared to be a main or major building flanked by a silo and a barn, both painted a stark combination of red and white. The central building wore a thatched roof. Its tiny windows contained colorful leaded glass. Smith estimated the height of the central building to be no more than three feet tall. Its brick walls and the flower boxes beneath each of its windows made him think of—. He sorted through vague images tumbling in his mind as Ashmadai chalked a fifth/on his scorecard.

Rachel's shocked cry reached him at the same moment that the sound of the explosion did. He gagged at the stench that filled the rotunda and stared in horror at the shattered body of the simulacrum lying on the floor. Smoke rose from it and from the ninth square where scarred and broken letters managed to say only:

COPENHAGEN

Ashmadai erased the marks he had made on his scorecard and opened the door of the closet containing the deactivated simulacra. He dragged a second one out into the rotunda. He propped it in place in front of the first square, twisted its dials, humming happily to himself all the time, and then returned to his position in front of the scorecard, chalk in hand, his oily tongue protruding between his teeth.

The second player succeeded in reaching only the seventh square before it and the letters designating *Orlando* were obliterated in a smoky burst of noise.

"Orlando gone," commented Ashmadai without emotion. "Copenhagen, too." He pulled down a map and next to the names of the dead cities wrote numbers. "Casualties," he answered when Smith asked him what the numbers represented. "They always occur. But I keep an accurate count of them. One must when one deals with hypotheses, so that when reality triumphs, as it sometimes does, one knows precisely how many dead to expect."

"Casualties," Smith said. "How many dead to expect. Not *who* died."

"I am a scorekeeper," Ashmadai snapped, "not a biographer."

"Rachel," Smith said, "we're leaving."

"But the game isn't ended!" Ashmadai protested. "Don't go yet. Stay and see whether anything survives."

"Your games don't interest me, Ashmadai," Smith stated. "Not anymore." Now what did he mean by that, he wondered, confused by his own words. Well, he had watched the game, on and off, for some time. He supposed that was what he meant.

"Where are you going?" Ashmadai shot at him.

"We're going back to the building where we——."

"Do you know the way back?"

"We'll find it."

"By Time: 110100?"

Rachel's hand tightened on Smith's.

He said, "What makes you smile, Ashmadai?"

"If you'll stay, I will introduce you to someone who can tell you the way back to the building you are seeking. He will save you time. As I said, I will introduce you to Loman if you will agree to stay—and play my game."

"I've seen what happens to those who play your game, Ashmadai."

"But you are a brave man, Smith. You are also, I imagine, one who is intelligent enough to know that barter is the basis of personal success. I offer you Loman's knowledge which you need in exchange for your cooperation so that I may thrill to the spectacle of flesh and blood, not just relays and analogues, risking self-sacrifice."

"What are the chances that I'll be killed if I agree to play?" Smith barked.

"The probability factors change each time there is a new player. I do not control them, I assure you. I merely service the control mechanism which is automatic once it is set in motion. One can never know while playing this game which of one's footsteps will cause the explosion that ends the game and oneself for good. A player can never know which—indeed, if any—squares are deadly. He takes his chances. I merely record the results of each game."

"You'll let Rachel go if I agree to play?"

Ashmadai laughed. "She is not my prisoner. She can go now, whether you agree to play or not. As a matter of fact, you too are free to go. No one is my prisoner here. Not even Loman."

Smith caught the glance Ashmadai hurled in the direction of the tiny house. "Loman lives there?"

"Yes. Will you play?"

"Smith, don't," Rachel pleaded. "We'll find the

building—."

"Before Time: 110100?" Ashmadai inquired, grinning blissfully.

"I'll play," Smith said and stepped up to the starting line. "Rachel, you'd better—."

"I'm staying."

"You see?" Ashmadai giggled. "What I told you is true. No one is my prisoner here. But everyone everywhere is someone's prisoner. Rachel is obviously yours, Smith, because she won't leave without you. I suppose she has her reasons.

"You are my prisoner—no, I'm not contradicting myself. You are my prisoner because you choose to be, not because I confine you physically. You are because you want something I can give you. That variable is the basis of any slave system. Even Loman remains over there in his domain within my larger one by choice. Loman is a prisoner of his own pain. Aren't you, Loman?"

Loman's voice responding to Ashmadai's shouted question was an already weak siren suffering the lack of amplification: "Every living thing is pain's prisoner. But I, in addition, was imprisoned by such shabby jailers as protocol and standard operating procedures."

Smith stood at the starting line of Ashmadai's game, listening to Loman's voice. Every word seemed to him tortured and accompanied by a barely heard sigh that was not only mournful but also angry.

Loman spoke a second time. "But I let myself be imprisoned. I thought that by so doing, I could change the system that allowed prisons such as the one I shared to exist. I was convinced that only inmates such as myself could alter the terrible conditions of the shameful prisons that contained them. No one outside such a prison, I believed, could exert sufficient influence or command prolonged attention. All those others had their own prisons, as you correctly pointed out, Ashmadai, and were therefore disinterested in mine."

Ashmadai clapped his hand and declared, "Loman loves to talk pompous nonsense. But he is sometimes entertaining."

"I talk truth," Loman protested, his tone still angry but edged now with urgency and no little sorrow. "If the truth I talk walks about your minds clothed in verbal baubles and articulate elegances, it is because such is the current fashion of truth-talking —a fashion, I must point out, which is commonly accepted, even applauded, in the palatial halls of power everywhere."

"Begin the game!" Ashmadai ordered impatiently. "I am not interested in listening to anymore ponderings. I have always been a man of intellectual action. Be silent, Loman!"

During his brief tirade, the simulacrum had crossed the rotunda and was kicking the walls of Loman's house to emphasize the earnestness of his order. Thatch from the roof drifted to the granite floor in a flaxen snow. When Loman became silent, Ashmadai grumbled his way back to his scorecard and peremptorily ordered Smith to move to the game's first square.

"Wait!" Rachel cried.

Smith kissed her as she ran into his arms but refused to heed her pleas.

"On with the game!" Ashmadai demanded. "The player does not need a coach, nor are strategic conferences in any way required equipment. The truly dedicated player needs only muscle, heart, and, most of all, balls! Begin!"

Smith whispered a final few words to Rachel and then shifted his position so that his hands were hidden from Ashmadai's sight. Leaning forward slightly, he dropped on the first square one of the heavy metal clasps he had taken from Rachel's gray gown.

When nothing happened as a result of his action, he stepped onto it. He began to talk to Ashmadai, his words spilling from his mouth without much thought or a great deal of order. He asked Ashmadai about the rewards of intellectual action. He expounded on the dangers of some games, and he called to Ashmadai to come closer to the mosaic and identify for him the name on the second square. He couldn't read it, he claimed. The sweat that was sliding down his forehead, he said, had entered his eyes and dimmed his vision.

Ashmadai, with evident reluctance, approached and squinted down at the floor. "The next potential disaster area," he told Smith, "is the country of Argentina."

Smith waited only another moment, just long enough for Rachel to drop to her hands and knees behind Ashmadai, and then he shot his fists forward to slam heavily against Ashmadai chest and chin.

An *aakkhhh* and Ashmadai was flailing about on the floor beyond Rachel over whose body he had fallen, propelled by Smith's blows.

Rachel sprang to her feet as Smith leaped from the game's squares and grappled with Ashmadai. Their battle was a brief one, Ashmadai using teeth and threats as he fought to free himself from Smith's grip. But Smith paid no attention to the teeth, which never touched his flesh, nor to the imprecations, which

169

could not weaken his determination.

"The rope!" he called out to Rachel. "I'll hold him while you tie it around his wrists. Make it tight!"

She succeeded in removing the knotted rope that circled Ashmadai's robed waist and, following Smith's directions, bound their prisoner's wrists.

When she had completed her task, Smith took the free end of the rope and tied it tightly to the iron post supporting one of the many torches lighting the rotunda. When he was satisfied with his efforts, he stepped back from Ashmadai who was bent forward, his head on a level with his navel, his arms were drawn up behind him by the rope Smith had used to bind them. He tried to turn, first one way and then the other, but the rope held and the angle of his arms kept him almost immobile.

"You cheated!" he screamed in fury at Smith.

"Was there a rule against a player quitting when he no longer wants to sacrifice himself in a ridiculous endeavor?" Smith asked innocently.

"Other players will call you coward!"

"Still other players will accuse you of common sense," Loman cried.

Smith went to the mosaic and retrieved the clasp he had taken from Rachel's gown earlier. He dropped it on the third square. When nothing happened, he repeated his action until he reached the sixth square, which exploded. Returning to Rachel, he said, "I just wanted to know when it would have happened. Somehow, I never actually believed that it would happen. I was tempted to keep on playing. I guess I wanted to win."

"You did," she told him. "You're still alive."

"And I'm still with you. You waited for me."

"Ashmadai was right. I couldn't leave you."

"Rachel, I—."

"Free me!" Ashmadai bellowed, straining against the rope. "The game—."

"Shut up!" Smith bellowed back, his fists clenched at his sides. When Ashmadai obeyed his order, he turned back to Rachel. "I don't remember ever feeling as deeply before about you. I think I know the word that fits my feeling."

Rachel said nothing.

"The word is 'love.' "

"I know."

"So do I," came Loman's small voice. "Come over here so that I can see you both."

Smith led Rachel to Loman's house and quickly knelt down to peer into one of its several windows. The colors in the leaded glass prevented him from distinguishing anything inside. Rachel, kneeling at his side, suggested opening the wooden door.

Using thumb and index finger, Smith turned the knob carefully. The door swung inward. "Loman?"

"Give me a moment. Wait for me."

As Smith and Rachel knelt in front of the house, they heard sounds of movement from within it. There was a creaking of springs and a wheezing sound of breath being drawn in pain. They both stared in shock as Loman dragged himself on hands and knees through the doorway to gaze up at them.

He wore a white terrycloth robe and black socks on his feet. There was a white bandage around his forehead. Above it, his lifeless brown hair swirled and below it was a ravaged face dominated by feverish eyes. He folded his arms and placed his head down upon them. The sound of his breathing wheezed softly.

"Loman?" Smith asked, watching the tiny figure,

which he estimated could measure no more than ten inches from the topmost strand of his unkempt hair to the soles of his feet.

"Yes, I'm Loman. Who are you?"

Smith introduced Rachel and himself.

"I'm very pleased to meet you both," Loman said and sighed.

"Is there something we can do for you?" Rachel asked him.

"To make you more comfortable?" Smith added.

"It's obvious that you two are in love with one another," Loman said. "Only people who feel love can care for others. Will you reach inside my house and bring out my chair?"

Smith carefully thrust his right hand through the low doorway and felt about inside the house until finally he touched a small chair, which he gingerly withdrew and placed to one side of the door.

"Please be good enough to place your hand here," Loman said.

"I'll lift you," Smith volunteered.

"No! I know you mean well. But you might crush me."

Smith placed his hand on the granite floor next to Loman who, by gripping the ridges of his fingers, was able to get to his feet. Holding onto Smith's wrist, he slowly made his way to his chair. When he reached it, he flopped down upon it with a faint moan.

"Thank you," he said after a moment.

Rachel glanced meaningfully at Smith.

He realized at once that she was waiting for him to question Loman about the location of the building they were both seeking. But he held back. The small simulacrum seemed so sick and in such pain that he felt guilty about asking for his help.

Rachel seemed to have sensed his feeling. She too refrained from asking the question that was on both their minds.

"I'm dying," Loman remarked matter-of-factly. "Did Ashmadai tell you that?"

Ashmadai let out a screech which was followed by, "Go back inside your shrunken world, Loman. It's your only chance for survival. I've told you that many damn times!"

"He's wrong," Loman said calmly. "I thought that by building this house, I might somehow survive. It didn't help. But, to begin at the beginning—you do want to hear my story, don't you?"

"We came to ask you a question," Smith blurted out.

"I will answer it if I can. What is it?"

Rachel said, "Tell us about your house, Loman."

Smith, catching her cue, inquired, "Why did you build it?"

"I know that's not the question you want to ask me. But I want to answer it anyway. I built my house because—. Can you imagine what it would be like to live in a world where other men cry 'vengeance' when you suggest 'amnesty'? I tried to dissuade Marsman from attacking the Valley of the Maimed. He spat upon me. I tried to point out to Professor Apocalypse that philosophy conceived to support an already designated end was not only bad philosophy but an intellectual obscenity as well. He simply said I was untrained in logic, which was true enough, I admit.

"Superstud told me he had no women of a suitable size for me. Borneo offered to exhibit me, but I could not be another man's toy. Helen of Troy found me impractical and Fantasia—well, Fantasia at least sympathized with my yearnings but she was occupied primarily with her own. Crutch—how he hated me because I was crippled—that is to say, a dreamer in a world of realists. Lord Ashmadai over there kept his most important games a secret from me.

"So I built this house to my measurements. I can sit on a chair in this house and eat from a table without feeling ridiculous. I can walk up two steps at a time in *this* house. I needn't battle ordinary staircases anymore. Now I sleep in a bed that is made to my measurements. But—."

"But what, Loman?" Rachel asked softly.

"But I sleep in it alone. I have built a universe scaled to my size, but in building it I have constructed my doom, since I must inhabit my world alone. My loneliness, I suspect, is the principal cause of the sickness that will one day kill me, although my memory tapes tell me that the diagnosis of an enlarged heart is not altogether faulty. The tapes tell me I am dying of a bad case, a fatal case, of virulent compassion accompanied by such dire complications as sincerity and unrealizable hopes."

"An incurable disease!" Ashmadai screamed. "I should never have let him come here. He may infect us all!"

"Men such as Ashmadai," Loman continued, unperturbed, "have always feared men such as myself because we threaten to break the rules of the games they love to play. But now I have told you my story and nothing has changed, has it? Neither of you are doctors, are you? In fact, you are not even like Ashmadai or Borneo or the rest of us, are you?"

"Rachel and I are human," Smith answered. "But —."

"I'm sorry," Loman said sincerely. "I didn't know you too were afflicted."

"Loman," Smith said, "can you tell us how to get back to the building which contains the crystal caskets—I mean—."

"I know the building of which you speak. And yes, I can tell you how to return to it. I will tell you. I would rather, I confess, invite you into my house to share another hour or two of conversation but that, as you can see, is impossible. So let me check my tapes. The directions should be there somewhere. All of us remember the place we were born and how to return to it, although most of us never really do return because we are far too busy blazing new trails to pay any attention to the ones we have already traveled."

"How can we find our way back?" Rachel asked anxiously.

"You could, of course, return to the surface and —."

"Time: 110100!" Ashmadai flung at them venomously.

Loman said, "Obviously, I must do what I must do. What my memory tapes tell me to do. I really don't need this house anymore in any case. I can lie anywhere—anywhere at all, while I wait for my heart to stop its needing.

"Behind my house is a passageway. It leads directly to a shaft that rises to the surface. At the top of the shaft you will find a trapdoor which you can raise and then you will find yourselves in the place you have been seeking."

Smith thought of the long journey through the tunnel that had at last led to the rotunda. We've traveled to the area directly beneath the big hall, he thought.

"Loman," he began, "can we move your house?"

Loman shook his head. "You will have to destroy it to reach the tunnel. I built the house against the tunnel in order to be close to those I remember caring about during our long association. It was a mistake, I suppose, given the present dilemma. But—just move me out of the way. Then demolition can begin."

"Isn't there some other way to reach the passage?" Rachel interjected.

"None," Loman replied. "Ashmadai would probably insist that destruction is a required prerequisite of progress. Perhaps he is right, although I for one always hated the concept. But bear the thought in mind as you break my windows and tear down the timbers under which I have unwisely been sheltering."

Smith looked at Rachel. "I have to do it," he told her. He bent and picked up Loman's chair and moved it and the tiny simulacrum sitting in it to a place safely distant from the house.

Then he kicked the house several times, gently at first, then more violently, so that it finally fell. The passage that was revealed by the collapse of the house was no more than three feet high.

"We'll have to crawl through it," Smith said to Rachel. "Do you think you can—?"

"I will."

Both of them turned back to gaze down at Loman, neither of them able to find the right words to frame their farewell.

"Goodby," Loman said. "It's really the only thing left to say. It always and ultimately is, you know."

"Goodby," Smith said.

"Thank you," Rachel said.

176

And then they dropped to their knees and crawled through the debris of Loman's house and into the dark tunnel, Ashmadai's voice ghosting after them.

"Help me, Loman!"

No reply.

"Loman, I will let you play all my games if you will but help me now! You always wanted to be more than just a bystander! You can be. I will even let you *win*!"

As Smith and Rachel continued crawling through the tunnel's darkness, they heard Loman's voice answer Ashmadai, but they could not distinguish his words.

Chapter 10

"RACHEL!" SMITH SAID as his hands found the first of the crude steps carved into the shaft that rose above him. "There's light up there."

Rachel crawled into the space he made for her by flattening his body against the wall of the passage. She stared up with him at the squared outline of light visible far above them.

Smith felt about in the darkness and announced, "These steps circle the shaft. There's no railing so we'll have to be careful. Are you ready to try it?"

"To be perfectly honest, I'm not. I'm afraid."

"I'll help you as we climb so that—."

"It's not the climb itself that frightens me. It's what we might find—what might happen to us when we get up there."

"Nothing will happen."

"You don't know that."

"Rachel, we have to find out what all this means. What Time: 110100 means and—."

"I know. I'm ready."

Smith began to mount the steps that were hidden from sight in the shaft's darkness. He ordered Rachel to hold his hand and to place her body as close as possible to the wall so that she wouldn't slip.

The sound of their breathing was audible as they

slowly mounted step after step, their heads bent backward as they kept the trapdoor and the thin line of light framing it in sight.

As they climbed, Smith repeated to Rachel that they were doing fine and that they would soon reach the safety of the hall. When she did not reply to the remarks meant to reassure her, he began to think of what might await them overhead. He imagined himself raising the trapdoor and climbing out onto the floor of the hall and then turning to help Rachel. Then they would—. His mind refused to offer him any possibilities. He wondered if he was afraid, as Rachel had admitted she was. He decided that, yes, he was, to some extent. But his fear was without focus. He wished that there was something known to which he could attach it. There was only the phrase *Time: 110100.* The time of their impending "disposition." But disposition by whom and for what reason?

As he continued his climb in the deep darkness around him, the shaft became his only world and he was gripped by a sense of unreality. Mechanically, he continued to place one foot in front of the other as the darkness around him blossomed with memories, which his imagination proceeded to embellish. He saw himself cavorting on soft grasses and in an aphrodisiacal air with female simulacra whose names were unimportant but whose bodies were treasure chests lavishly opened to him while Superstud stood nearby and talked of delights that never died. Helen of Troy beckoned to him, and as her mouth opened and closed, he heard her sad words and made promises in response to them. Crutch limped past them. High on a hill that was pinked with a rising but still unseen sun, Marsman girded himself for another battle, while far below, on a plain where broken bodies bled, Fantasia wove her tapestries of tender dreams. Borneo, at his workbench, built a devouring crocodile, while Professor Apocalypse lectured Loman on the dialectics of misplaced persons. Lord Ashmadai honed the blade of his long knife, his eyes seeking sacrifices.

The images vanished, the voices died, as Smith reached the top of the shaft. He placed his palms against the cold trapdoor above his head.

"Smith—wait a moment."

He understood immediately why Rachel had asked him to wait. There was something about the trapdoor —no, about the act of raising it, which he was about to perform—which would link two beginnings. One had occurred when he had first awakened in the room above him. The second was now, the moment in which he was about to return to that room. He thought of other beginnings—of himself and Helen of Troy. He thought about Rachel. It suddenly seemed to him that there were no actual endings. Endings were merely other beginnings. Everything, each experience, bore within it the seed of newness. The thought at first brought him pleasure. But as he considered its implications, he found that it also made him uneasy, because beginnings, once they were no longer seedlings, he had learned, ripened into trees that bore unpredictable fruit.

"I'm ready now," Rachel said.

Smith pushed against the trapdoor. It lifted. Light poured down upon him. He climbed up into the hall and turned to help Rachel mount the final few steps. A moment later, as she stood beside him, he noticed the dirt on her face and the way her gown was torn. He became aware of the gaudy clown's suit he still wore and which, like Rachel's gown, had been ripped in places and badly dirtied.

He spoke her name softly as he drew her up into his arms. He held her close to him for some time, unwilling to unmoor himself from her and to embark upon the sea of what he knew would be another beginning with an unforseeable end.

When they finally parted, he looked around the room. He was unable now, as he had been upon first awakening here, to locate the source or sources of the strong light filling the room. The glittering whiteness of the walls, ceiling, and floor seemed to be a part of the frosty light itself. His eyes wandered to the damaged door through which he had left the building earlier. He remembered the black bird that had been the first living thing he had seen upon awakening. Like him, it too, he recalled, had flown through the door that was still partially hidden from his sight by the wilted leaves drooping from the dying branches of the tree that had fallen upon it and forced it open. Like subtle and yet dominating elements of a landscape, the crystal caskets attracted his attention. He had been aware of them from the moment he had climbed through the trapdoor into the room. Despite the way their glassiness blended with the bland whiteness of the room in which they rested, he was keenly conscious of them and of the seven people they contained.

Seven people. Plus Rachel. And himself. Nine in all.

The number triggered a memory, which at first eluded him. But, after a moment of tense cerebral stalking, he captured it. The light screen had recorded that word, that number. *Nine,* it had said . . . .

Had he been avoiding a confrontation with the screen and the words it might hold—words he might not now want to read? He forced himself to turn around and face the screen.

It was blank.

No electric messages flitted across its face behind the protective glass that covered it.

Disappointment, a dull swamp of feeling, bubbled up within him as he stared at the empty screen. He knew the reason for his despair. He had wanted to see the words again now that he was no longer dazed and disoriented as he had been that first time. Then the message the screen presented had totally escaped him, enamored as he had been with the delightful flashings of light and not the meanings they conveyed. Now, he wanted to *know*. To know the meaning of this hall and the sleep he had experienced, the meaning of the simulacra and why he had met no other humans except Rachel in his recent odyssey, the meaning of that ominous phrase *Time: 110100.* He wanted—.

Rachel's sudden cry interrupted his thoughts.

He turned to her and then looked in the direction she was pointing.

The light screen gave off a soft glow. As they both stared at it, a familiar whistle sounded. The glow on the screen faded to a grayness bordering on blackness, and then, beginning at the left side of the screen and proceeding across it to the right and then on to an electric oblivion, marched words formed by dots of light.

Smith, standing rigidly with his eyes on the first of the words, was only partially aware of Rachel's harsh intake of breath and of her hand that gripped his own.

This message will repeat at regular intervals. Culture reconstruction continues via use of simulations of representative members of dominant surviving species of this planet, which is the third from its sun in a relatively stable system. Our chosen method, although necessarily somewhat symbolistic, is the only one feasible since all native artifacts have been destroyed. After identification via hypnotechnic interrogation, surviving specimens were placed in stasis to reduce risk of possible behavioral aberrations being manifested by them while our evaluation of the potential beneficence or deadliness of their species proceeds.

"Smith!"

"Wait! Look!"

Decision concerning disposition of nine to be determined based on evidence accumulated as a result of our electronic monitoring of the behavior and attitudes expressed by the simulacra, which we have modeled on Helen Macabe, Troy, New York; Bill Ketterling, Chattanooga, Tennessee; Bronson Laidlaw, Geneva, Switzerland . . . .

"Smith!"

He spun around in alarm at the sound of Rachel's ragged cry to find Marsman laboriously dragging the fallen tree away from the hall's doorway, a short sword clenched in his teeth, his eyes raging.

And then he quickly turned back to the screen.

. . . exclusive authority hereby granted to Survey Ship staff to make independent and unilateral decision concerning permanent disposition of nine based on data collected from the simulacra via your shipboard reception and storage unit. Your decision is scheduled for Time: 110100 after which you will return to fleet rendezvous coordinates outside planetary system now being researched.

"I declare war on you!" Marsman shouted as he stumbled into the hall. "On you, Smith, in particular, and on all humans in general!"

"The caskets!" Smith shouted to Rachel. "Get behind them!"

As Marsman advanced, he shifted his sword from his teeth to his hand.

Rachel ran behind the long line of caskets and crouched there.

Smith began to circle the room.

"I have come to return you to the sleep from which you escaped, Smith," Marsman muttered as he too circled the hall that had abruptly become an arena.

"Why?" Smith called out, keeping a safe distance from Marsman.

"Because I believe your wakefulness will cause my death. I weaken as you grow stronger. I believe that once your mind sustained me. Now it has deserted me, proving itself the traitor I always suspected it to be. I die, Smith, because you live!"

As Marsman circled warily, his sword glinting in the bright light, the diameter of the circle between himself and Smith diminished.

Smith's thoughts skittered through his mind. As he fought to seize and sort them, he realized that Marsman was behaving differently from the last time they had met. He became aware of the fact that the simulacrum's movements were less brisk now, at times almost spastic. Noting the effort with which Marsman performed even the simplest task, he realized that what Marsman had said—and what the screen had stated—was true. The simulacra were not only modeled on the humans in the room but were evidently activated by human emotions, thoughts, and memories.

"Marsman!" he flung at the simulacrum. "You're

nothing but an elaborate radio receiver that once utilized the electrical impulses from my brain. You were right when you said you're dying because I am living."

"I am a warrior!" Marsman retorted. "I obey orders. I fight. Enemies fear my mighty name and my obedient army!"

Smith sprang to one side as Marsman lunged. The sword in the simulacrum's hand flew harmlessly past the flesh it had sought to penetrate. As Marsman teetered, momentarily off balance, Smith spun around and gripped his wrist. He jerked it backward and then, using both hands, he flipped Marsman forward, sending him sprawling and knocking the sword from his hand.

"Go away, Marsman," he said softly, picking up the simulacrum's dropped weapon. "I don't want to kill you."

Marsman's eyes closed.

"But you will have to kill him," declared Lord Ashmadai as he climbed into the room through the open trapdoor, a burning torch in his hand. "Or else let him return you to silence and sleep so that he may survive."

"A simple but elegant equation," stated another familiar voice. "I should have solved it at the very beginning."

From the corner of his eye, Smith watched Superstud stride jauntily into the room.

"Enamored of numbers as I am," Superstud continued almost gaily, "I can now testify to the accuracy of Ashmadai's formulation."

Smith watched as Superstud crouched and then he stared in surprise at Crutch, who seemed to have materialized from nowhere. The single-legged simulacrum, he realized, had arrived borne on Superstud's strong back.

"We will not let you wake the others of your kind and thereby cause our deaths," Ashmadai intoned, obviously speaking for all the simulacra. "I have hired Marsman as a mercenary and summoned the others to prevent such a disaster."

"Crutch," Smith called out. "I never harmed you."

"The world has harmed me," Crutch answered bitterly. "And you are a part of that world. But I have my defenses, among which is my cherished hatred of you and your world."

The sound of the whistle's brief shriek startled Smith. He glanced at the screen and stiffened.

Time: 110042.

As the phrase fled the screen, a thin cry seeped into the room, causing Smith to turn. When his eyes met Rachel's, he nodded almost imperceptibly and received an answering nod from her. Their silent acknowledgment of one another seemed to state that mere machines could not defeat them. Neither of them gave any overt indication of their feelings concerning the knowledge they now shared—the disturbing knowledge that the machines threatening them both were something more than just machines.

The tiny cry came a second time.

"It's Loman," Rachel exclaimed.

Smith looked around, but Loman was nowhere in sight.

"Loman released me," Ashmadai declared. "He used his small but sufficiently sharp teeth to chew through the rope that held me prisoner."

Smith, remembering said, "Because you promised to—."

Ashmadai held up a hand. "He always yearned to play in my games. Now he can join us in this one, which we will all play together."

With a flourish, Ashmadai turned toward the open trapdoor.

As if waiting for just such a cue, Loman emerged from the hole in the floor, panting and obviously exhausted from his long climb up the steps that circled the shaft. "We can negotiate our differences," he shrilled excitedly when he had regained his breath. "Let us discuss coexistence."

As if his words were also a kind of cue, Marsman lumbered to his feet and struck a blow that sent Smith reeling backward.

Superstud caught him and flung him back into Marsman's arms.

Marsman gave an abortive cry. His arms released Smith. He clutched his abdomen.

Smith stared in horror as the simulacrum's knees bent and his body crumpled to the floor, the sword Smith had been holding in his hand jutting forth from the new home it had found. He started to speak, not sure whether he wanted to explain or express regret, but his words died as Ashmadai raced rapidly across the room toward him.

Smith looked to his left but Superstud stood there, smiling, waiting. Crutch, balancing on his one leg, raised his wooden limb.

"Rachel!" Smith shouted as he leaped across Marsman's unmoving body and seized the unattached conduit hanging from its duct in the ceiling. He tore it free and snaked it in a single whipping motion toward Rachel. She managed to catch its end and then, following Smith's shouted instructions, she ran along behind the caskets with it while Smith ran in front of them, the conduit stretched tightly between them.

The cable struck Ashmadai just below the level of his chest. As he toppled backward, his torch falling with him, Smith shouted an order to Rachel, and she released her hold on the conduit. He quickly knelt and wrapped it around Ashmadai's throat and pulled it tight. When Ashmadai's anguished eyes finally closed and his body no longer shuddered, Smith rose and stamped out the torch's flame.

And then he fell heavily as Crutch sailed his wooden limb through the air to crash against his skull.

"I'll let his woman know me!" Superstud exulted as he ran across the room. "Before I put an end to all her knowing!"

Smith, dazed, tried to rise from his knees. He wanted to call out to Rachel, but the words wouldn't come. He watched helplessly as Superstud lithely hurdled the casket behind which Rachel stood and seized her shoulders. Smith uttered an incomprehensible sound as Superstud bent his head and his open mouth trapped Rachel's.

When Superstud suddenly sank from sight, Smith managed to speak Rachel's name.

"I deactivated him," she stated tonelessly. "The dials behind his ears—I turned him off." She started to smile, but her smile never fully materialized.

Before she could shout a warning to Smith, he turned, alerted by her not-quite smile, to find Borneo bounding through the door and across the room toward him.

"Ashmadai was right, was right," Borneo sing-songed as he came closer. "When he asked me to help send you back to sleep, I told him I had circuses to impresario and many sundry and exciting toys to design. But he insisted I come, else all my circuses would be to no avail. He babbled something about the danger to us all should you awaken the others who still sleep here."

Smith backed away from Borneo, whose advance was forcing him back toward the line of caskets behind which Rachel was still sheltered. He looked about him for a weapon, but the only thing that might serve as one—the second detached conduit swaying in the slight breeze that had entered the hall with Borneo—was beyond his reach.

Borneo caught Smith's glance in the cable's direction and grinned, unexpectedly halting his advance. He reached inside his black coat and withdrew something, which he promptly dropped on the floor.

Smith looked down as the mechanical spider feathered its pink way on countless legs across the floor. A moment later, there was a second spider, this one a bright blue, gliding toward him. Then a third as pink as the first one.

Borneo's grin grew wider.

Smith edged to the left. The spiders hesitated and then they too altered their direction so that once more they were heading directly toward him. He moved rapidly away from them. As he did so, he noticed Borneo press a button on a small black box he had taken from his pocket. The spiders' legs blurred as the creatures increased the speed with which they were approaching their prey.

As he backed rapidly away from them, Smith stumbled over the fallen body of Marsman. Regaining his balance, he stepped over it, looking about him for some weapon with which he could smash the red-eyed arachnids that were closing in on him.

Frantically, Borneo pressed the button on his black box.

But he was too late. Two of the spiders collided with Marsman's body. Two explosions sent pieces of the simulacrum's body flying into the air. As the third spider also struck the same barrier, acrid gases billowed up from it, making Smith cough violently.

As his nostrils seared and the membranes of his throat grew agonizingly dry from the noxious gases that rose around him, he fought to remain conscious and on his feet. But his mind was unwilling or unable to control the movements of his body. He turned his head, stepped back, and drew several deep breaths. The gases still plumed about him, but he felt some brief relief from the little oxygen he had managed to inhale. Through dimmed vision he saw Borneo's grin, saw Marsman's mutilated body . . . .

He saw the battlefield that the hall had become shift and alter into something similar and yet not at all the same, as the gases muddled his mind.

Human bodies lay strewn on a vast flickering screen. That is the picture, he thought, his mind rocketing between the polarities of now and then, from the orbiting satellite that—. Around him panels flashed with little lights. Computers clicked. The clacking of a machine he could recall having operated sometime and somewhere spewed out a white worm of tape from its aluminum mouth.

In the center of the almost hallucinogenic blend of memories that the gases had brought rushing into his mind was his recollection of the assault bunker, that invulnerable sanctuary, miles below the earth, with its several layers of radioactive shields from which nine privileged people had—had—.

He staggered as the meaning of the row of red but-

190

tons he saw burst screaming into his thoughts. He wanted to call out to Borneo—to Arthur Dedham—and demand that no more buttons be touched. But he kept silent. As a Lieutenant Colonel in Amerland's Air Force, he was accustomed, conditioned, to obey the orders of his superiors however privileged might be his position as a member of Assault Team Exodus, and Arthur Dedham, nationally noteworthy thinker of the unthinkable, in his position as Rand Corporation theoretician, was unmistakably his superior.

Perhaps it was only the mind-altering effects of the gases. Or perhaps his changed perceptions grew out of a sudden new knowledge of what had happened to him since he had awakened and what was still happening to him. Perhaps he never spoke at all.

But someone spoke.

Someone's voice that sounded very much like his own screamed, *"Stop it!"*

Borneo simply kept on grinning.

While Helen Macabe, at her nearby desk above which hung a sign that said *Nuclear Control Center,* looked up in shock at the heretical sound of the scream.

Bronson Laidlaw placed a hand on Smith's shoulder and whispered words of consolation. "You should be able to stand it, young man. You are, after all, a soldier. I am only a refugee from my beloved Institute, a bought philosopher and consultant to Assault Team Exodus whose distinguished members pay no attention to my cant about the fallacies of a Nietzschean approach to Supermanhood."

Only Rachel Kerner, standing at her glass map on which missile trajectories were outlined and traced by moving electric lines, gave any indication of having understood the source of the painfully conscious scream. She drew a deep breath and returned her gaze to her map and its five white lines threading their way toward the land masses labeled *Eurounion.*

Smith shook his head. He rubbed his eyes. There was no map. There was only Rachel standing tensely behind the line of caskets in which—.

His own shout returned to him, rootless as an echo. But none of the sleepers heard it. All seven still slept. He looked from one to another of them, unaware of Borneo's surreptitious movement in his direction.

There was Carey Jones, Coordinator of the vast and largely secret network of Logistics Control whose birthday party he now recalled attending on a distant August sixteenth. Smith tore his eyes from the bearded man in the casket. There, too, he now understood, lay Carey Jones in the mechanical shape of the strangled Lord Ashmadai. Mathematician and amateur musician Bill Ketterling's handsome face, a neat network of flesh and features beneath his beard, was in the next casket. Smith remembered the man's actual sexual exploits with women less than he remembered Ketterling's endless boring boasting of his sexual triumphs, which were somehow linked to the numbers his mind loved to fondle. *Superstud!*

Smith heard the bitter voice of James Langley as he gave the final irrevocable order to launch the protective reaction strike against Eurounion. Gagging, Smith watched Langley lope about the assault bunker on the prosthetic device that had replaced the leg he had lost in an automobile accident as a child. Secretary of Defense James Langley. *Crutch!*

A silence.

A silence broken by the sorrowful sound of David Lowenthal's voice as he spoke to the determined pushers of buttons and to the eager watchers of screens where death indiscriminately harvested soldiers and civilians, women and children, water buffalo and mosquitoes, and all else without caring or counting. Lowenthal sounded like a man who knows his words are only words, perhaps destined to be published or quoted by newscasters, but incapable of ever interrupting the course of a single missile.

"I presented our policy at the United Nations," Lowenthal was saying, "as the President directed. I even tried to believe in it. But surely there is a saner way than this." He glanced up at the screen which showed a sky marred by missiles mindlessly pursuing their destructive destinies.

Smith became aware of Borneo's hands reaching through the eddying gases for his throat. Making an enormous effort, forced to move as if within an ocean, he managed to elude the simulacrum's grasp. He raised a foot and kicked out at Borneo. But he accidentally achieved a goal he had not sought. As his gaze lowered and Borneo's laughter raped his mind, he looked down and saw what his foot had unwittingly done to Lowenthal.

Loman lay writhing on the floor, his limbs convulsing, a ragged hole torn in his tiny chest.

Smith tried to speak, to explain to Loman that he had only been trying to protect himself from Borneo, that he hadn't meant to—.

But his words remained buried behind his numb lips.

Borneo raised his own foot and brought it down to cover and crush Loman's small body as it lay crumpled on the floor. "He was always a nuisance," Borneo commented, his foot completely covering Loman's body. "He was always asking questions. Too many questions altogether to suit the rest of us."

Smith's head gradually cleared as the last traces of the gases that had been released by Borneo's spider swirled away. But what he had seen and heard as a result of the effect of the gases upon his mind remained with him, and the awful knowledge of the holocaust and his own part in creating it followed in memory's painful wake.

When the whistle sounded, he hesitated and then glanced up at the screen.

Time: 110088.

Alarmed by the implications of the phrase as he now understood them, his eyes wishing to deny what they saw, he failed to hear Crutch's approach. The simulacrum halted and raised his crutch above his head. He began to whirl it about, a wooden bolo, and then he released his grip on it.

When it struck Smith, its impact sent him falling forward to collide with one of the empty caskets. He tried to seize it as it slid away from him, but he failed. It crashed to the floor, the sound of splintering glass drowning out the applause Borneo offered in recognition of Crutch's clever attack.

Rachel raced from behind the caskets and knelt down beside Smith, helping him to his feet. He eased her out of the way when he saw that Borneo had salvaged a long shard of glass and, holding it like a sword in both hands, was headed toward him.

He shouted to Rachel to run, knowing even as he did so that there was really nowhere for her to run, and then he began to sprint across the hall. He was almost halted in mid-stride by the idea that struck him. He wasn't convinced that it would work, but he had to try it. It was the only way he could think of to

194

defeat Borneo and Crutch, his only remaining enemies.

The thought flicked through his mind. *I am thinking like Marsman.*

Borneo pursued him about the hall as Smith taunted him. He shouted that Borneo was worse than a panderer. He had controlled Helen of Troy, Smith accused, and used her for his own purposes. An image of Arthur Dedham, the Rand Corporation theoretician, appeared to him. He thought of how Dedham's blunt judgments had always overruled Helen Macabe's equally blunt evaluations of the inherent dangers involved in Amerland's initiating a nuclear attack against Eurounion.

He halted.

Borneo, surprised to find his prey seemingly winded and waiting for him and the deadly lance he held in his hands, also halted. Then, his lips zipping open to reveal neat white teeth, he sprang.

Smith leaped away.

Borneo lunged a second time.

The open trapdoor, which he had failed to notice as he pursued Smith, tripped him and he fell. The sound of his cry diminished and finally stopped altogether as his body thudded to a final rest at the bottom of the shaft.

Crutch, who had been shouting encouragement to him, lapsed into a nervous silence as Smith reached out and tore the second unattached conduit from its anchorage in the ceiling duct. He snaked it out in front of him, using it as a whip, and began to move toward Crutch.

As Crutch hopped clumsily on his only leg toward the doorway, Smith cut him off. He snapped the whip in his hand. It sang its slick song, forcing

Crutch back into the center of the hall.

Smith regretted what he was doing even as he knew he must continue doing it. Watching Crutch's face twist in fear as his hands struggled to stave off the bitter kiss of the whip's tip, he placed one foot relentlessly in front of the other just as Crutch simultaneously hopped backward on his one foot in his retreat.

A final snap of the whip, and Crutch screamed. His hands flew up as his foot felt only air beneath it. He fell, still screaming, through the trapdoor and down the shaft to join Borneo.

Smith's arms dropped to his sides. His fingers relaxed their hold on the conduit and it fell from them. He lowered his head and closed his eyes. When he opened them a moment later, he looked about for Rachel.

Panic seized him when he could not locate her. He hurried over to the caskets, searching.

He found her lying behind them, unconscious.

As he knelt down beside her, he heard himself pleading with her not to leave him alone, not now. He bent his head and kissed her cheek.

Her moan as she regained consciousness was the most welcome sound he could recall ever having heard.

"Smith, before I fainted—I saw what you—." She closed her eyes.

A sharp sense of guilt overcame him. "Rachel, I had to do it."

She looked up at him. "I know. We do what we think we must do."

"Then you remember too," he said, certain that her last remark meant that she too had finally recalled the time preceding their casketed sleep.

"Remember? No. Do you?"

196

He told her everything he had remembered, everything except the one thing that was still lost to him—his name.

She listened without asking any questions or making any comments until he had concluded his explanation of what they each had done to cause their present predicament.

She said, "What time is it?"

He glanced at the blank screen. "I don't know."

She dropped her head into her hands after sitting up. "They have no right, whoever they are! It isn't fair! How can they possibly *know*?"

"Know what, Rachel?"

She uncovered her face. "What it's like to be human. We know now that they're not. So how can they know about—about the fears that drive us to desperate acts or our struggle to conquer those fears. How can they possibly know? Because they can't know, they have no just basis on which to condemn us."

Smith knew he had to say what he was thinking, although he knew also that it would offer Rachel little consolation and not much more hope. "If you try to see things from their point of view, whoever they are and regardless of the fact that they are not human, it seems clear to me that they had little choice but to do what they did to us. They found us —the nine of us who survived the start and almost simultaneous end of World War Five—and they didn't know what had happened, although they certainly must have seen the devastation. In fact, the screen mentioned the destruction of all our artifacts. But they didn't know anything about our species. They were suspicious of us and rightly so, based on what Earth must have looked like to them when they arrived. It must have resembled a cemetery."

"Yes, a cemetery. It had to be one if we were the only survivors."

"Because of their suspicions about us, they put us into stasis after subjecting us to interrogation under something they call hypnotechnic, as the screen said, to find out who we were and to activate our—well, our dream lives. They did so because they thought we might be dangerous to them should we ever reach their world, wherever it may be. Then they built the simulacra which they activated through the transmission of the electrical impulses from our nine brains. The simulacra—their speech and behavior, even the names they chose for themselves—were reflections of ourselves—both our conscious and our unconscious thoughts, desires, memories, and wishes. So now, whoever they are—they know a great deal about us."

"But they don't know everything," Rachel protested. "They don't know about you and me, for example. I mean about human love."

"Human love," Smith repeated, a note of scorn sharpening his tone. "Rachel, I told you that I remembered being an officer in our Air Force. A warrior like Marsman," he added. "Set that fact against my demonstrated but erratic capacity for love and —."

He picked up a piece of glass that had once been part of the casket in which he had slept and strode briskly across the hall to where Marsman's body was lying. He sliced open the simulacrum's forehead and stared down at the engraving on the gold plate that was riveted to the machine's metal skull.

"Smith?"

He returned to where Rachel stood waiting for him. "My name," he said. "It's Steve Petry."

198

"Steve. Steve Petry." She reached up and touched his face gently.

They were silent for a moment and then Rachel said, "There are good things about being human. Steve, there *are*!"

"Helen's admirers murdered her," he mused aloud. "They didn't give her a chance to die in peace."

"She was a machine!"

"She was Helen Macabe."

"But—," Rachel began, glancing into the casket in which Helen Macabe lay sleeping. "But she's so—unattractive."

"Maybe that's why she hated men so much," Steve suggested. "She often said she did."

"An unattractive woman who hated men. Then how could Helen of Troy who was so beautiful and so seductive be a—a construct based on Helen Macabe?"

Steve hesitated in the face of Rachel's continuing attempt to deny the truth of what they had discovered. Briefly, he considered remaining silent. But he couldn't because, he believed, the truth had to be told. Now was no time for lies.

He said, "I remember going to Helen's room one time. I can't remember exactly why I went now, but I know it had something to do with our need for the figures she was preparing on possible overkills as a result of our planned assault. I knocked, and her door which was ajar swung open. She wasn't there. I noticed some magazines on the table just inside the room. They were nudist magazines."

"Probably none of us were puritans."

"The nudes were all male," Steve said, and watched understanding shadow Rachel's face. "Obviously, Helen of Troy reflected the sexual fantasies and carefully hidden desires of Amerland's most renowned nuclear physicist—Helen Macabe's lusts."

"But what about Loman?" Rachel cried, a note of desperation sounding deep within her voice. "He was so gentle!"

"So was David Lowenthal. He tried so hard to make peace in his capacity as Amerland's UN representative—right up, in fact, to the last too-late moment. Crutch, remember, willingly sold his blood to the highest bidder at the circus. Consider me, Rachel. I killed several of the simulacra. Marsman killed countless numbers of them in the Valley of the Maimed."

"But what you did you did in self-defense!"

"Lord Ashmadai was modeled on Carey Jones of Logistics Control. He sacrificed Professor Apocalypse. That wasn't self-defense. That was the triumph of technology over thought."

"But Loman!" Rachel argued. "He *loved*!"

"Do you remember what he said? He said, 'I tried to point out to Professor Apocalypse that philosophy conceived to support an already designated end was not only bad philosophy but an intellectual obscenity as well.' Even our resident philosopher, Bronson Laidlaw, who gave birth to the Professor out there, lent his talents to the support of our appetite for slaughter. I didn't understand what Loman meant at the time he made that remark. I do now. You say that David Lowenthal sought peace, that he loved. But if Ashmadai's comment, which could only have come from the knowledge possessed by Carey Jones, was correct, then Loman-Lowenthal wasn't altogether untainted either. He was, after all, a member of Assault Team Exodus, just as you and I were."

"What remark are you referring to?"

"Ashmadai said that Loman had always wanted to play in his games. That's the prize Ashmadai promised Loman in return for his freedom. He offered Loman a chance to belong if Loman would free him, and Loman accepted the offer."

"But they were all only machines!"

"Yes, they were. But you know that they were also all of us, Rachel. We have to face that fact." He frowned. "They said so many things that puzzled me at the time they said them. I wish I could remember them all now. I didn't understand the real significance of much of what they said at the time they said it, but now I know that they were revealing us to ourselves, and neither they nor we quite realized it at the time."

Steve stopped talking as his ears detected a faint hum which he could not identify but which nevertheless thoroughly alarmed him. "We're not the ones who will decide our future—if we're to have one," he said.

Almost before he had completed his statement, the hum he had heard matured into a deafening roar.

Outside the hall where night was falling, a blue star that was not a star glowed.

Rachel moved closer to Steve as they both stared apprehensively through the open doorway.

The roar ended and so did the bright blue light as the stark needle of the ship landed outside the hall.

They kept their eyes on it as the door in its side slid open and then Rachel cried, "Steve! We've forgotten about the others!" She hurried across the hall toward the row of caskets. "We have to wake Helen and David and—!"

"No!" he stated firmly as he caught up with her and took her arm. "Let them stay asleep."

She studied his face for a moment before speaking. "You believe that it might be better for them if they don't know what—."

"Yes," he interrupted. "I do."

The familiar whistling shrilled.

As it did, Steve and Rachel turned to confront the first of the many inhuman beings who were entering the hall. And then they reached out their hands to each other, ignoring the screen and the single phrase that blazed briefly upon it:

Time: 110100.